Dixie White and the Seven Dates

By

Cat Shaffer

DEDICATION

To my friend M.J., veterinarian extraordinaire: here's the rest of the story.

Chapter One

Michael was drunk.

And Dorothea was hiding behind a potted palm in Chicago's most exclusive country club listening to her boyfriend of six months trash her.

"The most attractive thing about her is the money." He formed the words with care, as if to make sure they didn't slur. "The old man's connections and his huge piles of cash are going to put me in the governor's mansion."

A leafy frond kept Dorothea from seeing Michael's conversation partner. But she could hear quite well as his male companion asked, "So that makes up for her being a flat-chested daddy's girl with the personality of mashed potatoes?"

"Hell yeah." Michael laughed. "All she has to do is stand behind me and pop out a baby at the right time. Her father thinks I'm golden. As long as I protect his precious little girl from the big bad world, I can do anything I want."

Dorothea grasped a thick stem and squeezed, the same way she wanted to put her hands around Michael's worthless neck. He was such a good liar. She'd believed he actually loved her.

That she was a refreshing change from the shallow, flashy women he dated before.

Refreshing. Right. He meant sheltered and too blind to see him for what he was.

Footsteps coming her way reminded Dorothea her hiding place was next to the women's restroom. She did not need anyone from Dad's party seeing her huddled here. She took a deep breath, squared her shoulders and retreated to the safety of one place she knew Michael couldn't go.

She stared at herself in the restroom mirror. She wasn't ugly. Then again, she wasn't beautiful. Her slim navy sheath dress was a classic. The pearls she wore at her neck and ears were a gift from Dad and her favorite piece of jewelry. She'd pulled her dark hair into a chignon tonight, only a slight change from the way she usually wore it, clasped at the back of her neck with a wide barrette.

Michael was right. She was nothing without Daddy. The only jobs she'd ever had were summer internships during college, but those were through friends of her father, one with a brokerage firm and in another's bank trust department. The degree in

English and women's studies she acquired at a top-notch all-women's school turned out to be useless in the real world. But since she expected to live at home until she married and serve as her father's hostess at the many functions he sponsored, career planning wasn't high on her list of priorities then.

Or now. She turned on the taps and washed her hands, avoiding her face in the mirror. Her mother's death from cancer when Dorothea was two created an extremely close relationship with her father. The need to remember their position in society kept her from questioning things. The rarified world of private schools, old money families and maintaining a pristine reputation at all costs created a perfect conformist who not only wouldn't rock the boat, but wouldn't even go near it.

Which means Michael is right. I'm a mousy little nothing.

She took a deep breath, dried her hands on the soft towel an attendant handed her and prepared to rejoin the party. January tenth was a special day. That's when Daddy threw a huge fête for everyone in the law firm to celebrate yet another good year. The anniversary of being made partner in his late father-in-law's practice caused him to be almost mellow. Tonight he'd reminisce, drink too much of the celebratory champagne and probably announce a new partner.

Michael, no doubt. He and Daddy had been in quiet discussion off and on during the evening. Much as she'd like to tell the jerk she overheard every word he said, her father would never forgive her for making a scene on his big night. She'd stand beside Michael tonight, act thrilled when Daddy made the announcement and begin refusing all his calls in the morning.

"There you are, darling." Her father approached as she walked back into the massive ballroom. The dimmed crystal chandeliers were turned up. Time for the big declaration, she supposed.

Tucking her hand into the crook of his arm, she walked to the small stage and waited while the musicians finished their song. When they left for a break, she followed her father up the steps to the center microphone. The practiced smile stayed on her face as she stood, head tipped as if she was listening, while he launched into a speech about what a great year it had been and how he appreciated everyone's hard work. Then came the moment Dorothea expected.

"It's hard to believe it's been nearly thirty years since I became a part of Pendergraff, Holmes, Meecham and Pfister," he said. "Back then, with this beautiful young woman still in a crib, I worked the long, hard hours it takes to be a success in this business. Over those decades, I've watched other young men and women follow that same path. So tonight, I'm pleased to announce that one of those hard workers, Michael Butterwell, is becoming a partner."

Dorothea applauded along with everyone else. She managed not to pull back when Michael bounded up to join them and planted a kiss on her cheek. His whiskey breath about knocked her out. Her father must have noticed; she wondered what he thought.

She held the pose of beaming girlfriend as Michael made a short speech of gratitude and promised to live up to the honor he'd been given. The smile slid from her face when her father took the microphone back and said, "I consider you all my friends, and I'm glad you could join me for another momentous moment. Michael?"

The crush of people around the modest platform kept her from running when the rat dropped on one knee, took her hand and—staring straight into her eyes—said, "Dorothea Pfister, will you do me the honor of becoming my wife?"

No. Oh, God no.

The refusal stuck in her throat when she made the mistake of looking at her father. The man who gave her everything she wanted and so much more was tearing up. He'd never done that before.

She glanced at the assembled family and friends. Rejecting Michael's proposal would crush Daddy. She did what a good girl should.

She smiled and held out her left hand. Michael slipped on a diamond ring that must have cost a fortune but felt like shackles.

"I believe Dorothea's too overcome with emotion to speak," her father said, clearing his throat and brushing at his right eye. "I will tell you that a fall wedding is in the works. I trust you can join us again for their engagement party in early spring."

The band came back, Michael led her to the dance floor and Dorothea found herself the center of attention. She hated being stared at, especially now when she was acting out the biggest lie of her life. She didn't want to waltz with Michael, his hot breath stinking against her face. She wanted to run back to the house, hide in her room and pretend this night had never happened.

"May I cut in?"

Her father made a smooth exchange. His face wore a giant smile.

"Surprised, honey?"

"Totally."

"Michael asked for your hand last week. We decided this was the perfect time for a proposal, with everyone who matters here." He squeezed her hand. "That young man is going places. I won't have to worry about you being taken care of when I'm gone. Your mother would be very happy."

"I simply can't believe he proposed." She was not about to discuss her unwanted fiancé's suitability as a husband.

"Patrice has started plans for the engagement party. I've booked the hotel ballroom and she's meeting with the caterer on Monday. I believe she's in touch with a music combo as well."

Of course Patrice was on top of things. She started as Daddy's executive assistant two years after Dorothea's mother died, and gradually began to run his life. The arrangements of red roses on the tables, the flowers of romance, were probably the woman's nod to the surprise proposal.

"Do we have to rush things?" Dorothea tried to hide the panic she felt. "It's not like we have to hurry with a wedding."

She was answered with a *father knows best* smile.

"Timing is everything," he said. "Patrice likes the early spring party because it's ahead of the rush of May bridal showers and June weddings. Since I only have one little girl, I want her to get all the attention she can."

He dropped a kiss on the top of her head.

"I'm proud of you, dearest, and love you very much."

The music stopped. Michael rushed up as if she might escape and put an arm around her waist. When he spoke, the stench of whiskey was even stronger. How did she miss his love of liquor?

Well-wishers thronged around them, eager to examine the rock on her finger.

"Absolutely stunning," gushed the woman Dorothea had been taught to call Aunt Abigail. The wife of another senior partner, she never failed to mention Dorothea's resemblance to her late mother. She pulled the ringed hand closer for a tighter inspection.

"Emerald cut center diamond, perfect sapphires on each side and heavens, those small diamonds circling the band are exquisite. I'll have to ask your young man if he had it designed at Alejandro's."

Dorothea felt like an unpaid hand model by the time everyone looked their fill. Only Aunt Abigail was bold enough to come right out and talk about it. Dorothea had the uncharitable thought that her father might have footed the bill for it. She suspected Michael wouldn't have spent thousands from his own bank account considering what he thought of her. And Daddy would want her to have the best.

"You look tired, sweetheart." Michael ran a finger down her jaw. "I have to stay until the last stuffed shirt leaves, but you can go home anytime.

The exciting part's over anyway." He motioned to her father before she could stop him.

"Dorothea's ready to go home," he said, as if she wasn't even standing there. "The evening's been a lot for her. I don't want her overstressed."

He disappeared to retrieve her mink. Her father took Michael's words as gold, hugging her in farewell and turning her over to Patrice when the other woman offered to drive her home.

"Here you are, darling." Michael stumbled as he walked up to help Dorothea into the fur coat. He kissed her before she realized his intent, leaving the taste of whiskey on her lips. She glanced over her shoulder as she left the ballroom and wasn't at all surprised to see that he'd joined the obviously drunken blond law clerk.

The biting winter air chilled her face as they waited for the valet to bring the car around.

The bare trees lining the circular drive suited her mood perfectly in the stark bleakness.

Dorothea leaned her head against the soft leather of the headrest as they headed away from the club and closed her eyes. My heavens, what a mess!

"You're a lucky woman." Patrice's voice came from the darkness. "Most young men these days want a wife with skills of her own. Michael seems quite content to handle everything and give you adequate staff. Your marriage will be so good for your father as well. Victor has put his own wants and needs on hold since your mother's passing to give you a nice upbringing.

Now he can have a life of his own after all this time."

The tension headache that began when Michael dropped to one knee was becoming a thumping monster. Still, it wasn't bad enough for Dorothea to miss the message. *She* was the albatross around her father's neck.

Patrice should know. She had wormed her way into the Pfister household. Dorothea might serve as hostess, but Patrice organized every dinner party at the house. She made sure the decorators came on Thanksgiving weekend to dress up the house for Christmas. Dorothea also had a feeling she arranged for the gifts Santa brought during her childhood.

She opened her eyes as Patrice drove around the large house and into the attached four car garage. She wanted nothing more than the refuge of her room and the chance to take off the rock weighing down her hand.

What she got was another lecture thinly veiled as reassurance.

"I hope you understand what a large undertaking a wedding is," Patrice said. "Don't worry, though. Your father intends to spare no expense, and I'll make sure everything is right. The best thing to do is relax and start looking at houses.

I've already given your young man a realtor recommendation and the name of several good designers. I think you two would be quite happy in one of the new developments on the edge of the city."

"Can we talk in the morning? My head is aching terribly."

"Of course, dear." Patrice was immediately solicitous. "Shall I have some milk warmed for you?"

"No, thank you," Dorothea answered, wondering if she sounded as awful as she felt. "I just want to go to bed."

Sleep was bound to help her head. Once the little guys with drums quit marching inside her brain, she might be able to concentrate on something other than the pain.

Like an escape plan.

That was her last thought before she fell into the worst night's sleep she'd had in ages.

Morning came too soon, in the form of Patrice marching into her room after a perfunctory knock. The older woman carried a thick ring binder in one hand and a glass of orange juice in the other.

"Good morning, dear." She handed over the juice before taking the chair at the glass topped dressing table. "I hope you're feeling better."

Patrice flipped over the binder and began talking before Dorothea could say yes, no or thank you. And kept talking, much to Dorothea's dismay. The cold juice was the only good thing about the next hour.

"I'll be consulting with your father." Patrice shut the binder with a bang. "And your fiancé, of course. All the appointments should be booked by the end of the week. Oh, yes, a personal trainer will be coming to the house to work with you. You need to be as slim a bride as possible.

"Now why don't you get dressed and come downstairs? Several congratulatory flower arrangements have already arrived."

As soon as the door shut behind Patrice, Dorothea groaned and slid down in the bed, covering her head with the comforter. The night's stress dreams were nothing compared to the nightmare inside that binder. Enduring some stranger coming to the house to measure her in her underwear for a custom wedding dress was bad enough. The idea of sweating with a trainer and spending a week at a spa getting beautiful before the engagement party crossed the line.

Bravery was hers as long as she huddled in her safe nest. She mentally worked and reworked what she would say when dumping Michael and the explanation she'd give Daddy. She began to doubt herself as she dressed. By the time she saw the first vase of flowers on the sideboard, she knew resistance was useless. Her life was out of her control like a raft drifting out to sea.

"A visitor, miss."

Brenda, one of the downstairs staff, interrupted her breakfast in the sunroom. Dorothea took one more quick bite of her egg white omelet before rising with reluctance to greet the newcomer.

One look into the formal sitting room confirmed her worst fear. There stood Michael, arms outstretched as if he expected her to run right into them. She wanted nothing more than to run the other way. Pretending she didn't know he was waiting for a hug, Dorothea pasted on a smile and invited him to join her.

She tried to listen when he talked, but it all sounded like *blah blah blah*. The redness of his eyes and the bags underneath them were telltale signs he had done some hard celebrating after she left. Too bad he hadn't stayed home to recover.

"You're lucky to have someone like your father's assistant to take over."

That penetrated the fog. Lucky? More like cursed, considering her future was outlined in pages of notes in that blasted blinder.

"Yes, Patrice is one of a kind," she said at last.

"We'll have to see if she'll still be your advisor after we're married." Michael filled his coffee cup. "You don't want to handle those hard decisions."

"Like what?"

Michael frowned. "You know, what clubs to join, scheduling lunches, things like that. The sort of stuff that will make you a good wife for my career."

Egotistical jackass.

Dorothea wished she had the courage to say those words out loud. But she hated confrontation. Calling him names would certainly lead to conflict. So she nodded as if every word he said was golden and wondered why she hadn't taken practical courses in college. Like how to turn invisible when life went completely insane.

"Wear that blue dress, the one with the swirly stuff at the neck."

"What?" She had once again missed what he said.

"Tomorrow night. When we meet my parents for dinner. Maybe you can do something different with your hair too since we're celebrating."

Noooooo! Not dinner with his parents. Or him ever again for *that matter.*

She had to stop this right now. Give back the ring. Tell him good luck, and no hard feelings. But he had already made *arrangements* with his parents. Cancelling would be so rude.

Her headache came back full force as the morning wore on. Patrice called twice, first to tell her an appointment for her engagement photo had been set and the second time to inform her a duplicate binder was being made so they were on the same page at all times.

When she ran into Brenda on her way back to her suite, Dorothea did something she'd never done before. She asked an employee her opinion.

"What do you think of Michael?"

The *deer in the headlights* look Brenda took on gave her the answer despite the maid's careful response.

"He's an attractive man."

She didn't like him either.

With a "Yes, he is," Dorothea continued on her way. Behind the closed door of her room, she studied the ring on the dresser top. She should be thrilled to wear it. Any other woman would. Michael had many good qualities. He was ambitious, dressed well and fit in everywhere he went. If she hadn't overheard him last night….

But she had. She couldn't forget he only saw her as the means to a high-powered and influential end. She sighed. Her life would be so much easier if she could just disappear.

Hmmm. Maybe she could, at least for a little while. The vacation condo in Miami was empty. Daddy would understand if she wanted a little time to herself. A week or two away would be long enough to come up with some sort of plan to get out of this predicament. Her confidence restored, she called his office.

Their conversation added to her depression.

"Really, Daddy, you don't need to go with me. The travel agency can take care of everything. I hate for you to rearrange things at the office just for me." She listened a moment and then answered, "I understand. We can talk about this later."

Dorothea ended the call and tossed the phone on the bed, dropping on her back beside it.

Laying there staring at the elaborately plastered ceiling, she realized how sad her life was. Nobody loved her like her father, and even he thought she was too incompetent to fly to Miami and stay in the house all by herself.

She couldn't be *that* useless. Absolutely couldn't.

The time had come to prove it.

Before she could succumb to second thoughts, she went to the walk-in closet and found a tote bag. She put in clothing for a couple of weeks, added her toothbrush and deodorant and stuck in nightgown and slippers. With a casual stride, she headed down to Daddy's study, opened the secret part of his desk drawer and pulled out a banded stack of cash. That couple thousand and her no-limit credit card should get her to Florida. A deep breath later, she had the keys to the Saab in her hands. Stopping in the kitchen, she told the housekeeper she was going out and didn't expect to be home for dinner.

Exhilaration filled her as she backed out of the garage. Adventure was hers. For the first time in her life, she was breaking the rules.

At the end of the cobblestone drive, she stopped and looked for traffic. A right turn would take her to the freeway and on to the airport. A left turn would take her...

She didn't know. Away from this house and Michael. Away from Patrice and all her plans. Even away from Daddy and his patronizing manner when she suggested she fly by herself.

She hit the gas and headed left, into the unknown.

Toward a place where no one knew her name, no one cared if she failed.

Toward freedom.

Chapter Two

One mindless turn after another led Dorothea to the interstate and another choice. Should she join the steady flow of vehicles or turn around and go home?

Either way was a step into unknown territory. She hadn't been gone long. No one would have missed her yet. Not even Patrice, who apparently told her father everything. But she wouldn't be the same woman who left. Going back meant finding a way to dump Michael, a confession to her father why she'd done so, and who knew what consequences after that. She never wanted to see Michael again, but she didn't want to get him fired or trash his reputation. No matter what she did, her life would never be the same.

If she kept her foot on the gas and her eyes on greener pastures, she would have to fend for herself. A whole new world lay out there, one without her comfortable room and a staff that made sure everything was as it should be.

As her car drew up to the on-ramp, she pushed down the gas pedal and made the merge. She needed to regroup and recuperate from the blows to her ego. She couldn't do that in the house that Daddy built.

Dorothea settled into an easy pattern after a few miles with cruise control set and the radio rolling out soothing classical music from a station she'd accidentally found. She was doing okay until an older sedan blew past her with the words *Just Married* written on the back window.

She began to cry.

The tears came easily. By the time an exit loomed, she was sobbing and desperately needed to get off the road. She took the exit and drove into the parking lot of a huge building marked Walmart. Surely she could find tissues there.

She found a space near the wide glass entrance and scrubbed her face with her hands in an attempt to look somewhat presentable. She'd seen these stores before but never been in one. Shopping was something done for her, not an activity she undertook herself. And certainly not in a place like this where pick-up trucks and SUVs filled the parking lot.

Dorothea walked through two sets of double doors and stopped in her tracks. The place was huge and busy.

"Need a buggy, honey?"

A woman in a blue smock pushed a metal shopping cart toward her. Dorothea took it; she would hate to offend the woman. She dropped her leather purse in it and joined the throng, relieved to find a stack of tissue boxes lined up with other merchandise flanking the entry. The price astounded her. It was so cheap she took a dozen boxes.

Venturing further on, she saw a display of children's clothing and another woman in a smock.

"Excuse me," she asked the smiling smocked worker, "where would I find your spring transitionals?"

"You mean mowers and stuff?" The woman waved toward her left. "They'll be in lawn and garden."

"Uh, no, clothing. The sort that you wear from one season into the next."

"Oh, honey, the cute stuff has just come in. Go down two aisles, swing a right and you'll find your size."

Dorothea followed the casual instructions to find rack after rack of clothing of all sorts.

Winter coats with a clearance sign hanging above them were sleeve to sleeve with pastel blouses. Bright colored skirts beckoned along with shelves and shelves of jeans. Hanging tightly to her cart, she went to investigate.

Good heavens, they were practically giving these clothes away. She could have an entire wardrobe for less than she usually spent on a nice dinner. She grabbed this, picked up that and soon had her cart half-full. She finished filling it up with a trip through the shoe department and what was quaintly labeled health and beauty. Several hundred dollars later, she had her arms full of bags and a new sense of accomplishment. Who knew shopping could be enjoyable?

"Looks like you bought out the store."

The comment came from a young woman sitting on a bench by what appeared to be a hair salon.

"I couldn't decide so I took it all," Dorothea answered.

"Maybe you need a new look to go with it," the woman suggested as she stood. "We've got great specials on cuts and color today. I can take you now."

Dorothea patted the knot at the back of her neck. She kept her hair long because Daddy liked it that way. Michael, too.

The very thought of the rat made her follow the woman into the small salon.

"I'm Julie by the way." Her new hairdresser patted a chair. "Sit down and let me see your hair."

Dorothea unpinned the clasp of the barrette and let her hair fall, watching herself in the mirror. She usually saw it as a glorious waterfall. Today it looked old-ladyish.

"Cut it off."

"You're sure about that?" Julie tipped her head and studied Dorothea. "I can trim and shape it a little and you can still keep the length."

"Make it short." Michael would have a cow when he saw her. Daddy might too, but hair grew back. "Like here."

She gestured to a place right below her ears.

"You're sure?" Julie asked again.

"Positive."

In less time than she would have imagined, her long locks were lying on the floor. Dorothea swung her head, thrilled by the look of her new bob and the dramatic feeling of freedom from losing all that heavy hair.

"What else can I do?"

"Anything you'd like."

"How would I look as a blonde?"

She swiveled the chair to address Julie.

"Too bold. Won't match your coloring. How about some highlights a shade or two lighter?"

"That will be fine."

Dorothea listened to the hairdressers chat with their clients as Julie went to work on her hair. Their lives sounded challenging, but everyone seemed happy. Could she make the same kind of life for herself?

Patrice certainly didn't think so. Of course, neither did Michael. And honestly, if she'd had a handkerchief in her purse, Dorothea would probably have turned around and headed home by now, her rebellion over. Gone home and studied her boring wardrobe for the right dress for dinner with Michael's parents.

"No." She didn't realize she spoke aloud until Julie froze and lifted her hands into the air.

"Too much?" the hairdresser asked.

"Sorry, thinking out loud." Dorothea offered her most sincere smile. "I like what you're doing. I think it will look quite nice."

"Me too." Julie dabbed goo on a few more pieces of hair. "I'm going to let you sit for a while, and then we'll wash it out."

Dorothea found a chair and picked up a magazine. She tried to read an article about skin regeneration products but couldn't make sense of it. Her mind was abuzz with possibilities.

She didn't have to go home today. The money she had taken for her airline ticket and limo to the Florida place should finance a couple of days in a nice hotel. She'd sleep in, order room service and try to find a way out of the dreadful situation in which she found herself.

"Ta-da!" Julie turned the chair around with a flourish. Dorothea stared into the mirror at the results. She barely recognized the woman looking back at her.

"You are a magician," she said.

"Because you're a dream to work with. I gotta say, though, this is quite a transformation. You're leaving a new woman."

Elation filled Dorothea as she paid Julie, adding a generous tip, and left the store with her purchases. She could do this.

The Saab hummed along at the speed limit, seventy miles per hour with cruise control set, as Dorothea headed south on the interstate. When her stomach rumbled, she pulled into a rest area to eat the pre-made sandwich she purchased at the store's deli section. She was surprised at how fresh and tasty it was. She finished her impromptu meal with a soft drink and cupcakes from the vending machines.

The miles slid past as she got back on the road and kept driving. She switched from one super highway to another, caught in traffic, and was surprised to see a Welcome to Kentucky sign. She was hungry again, it was getting late and she supposed she needed to figure out how to find a hotel.

Louisville, she discovered, was a busy and confusing city. So she stayed on the interstate until the city was behind her and her stress level went from the red zone to nearly normal. When an Exit Ahead sign loomed, she decided to get off and take her chances. Perhaps she'd find something suitable there.

Neon shimmering in a diner window jumped through the dusk at her. The sign out front advertised home cooking and a number of vehicles were in the parking lot. She pulled in and joined them.

The place was small inside but filled with conversation and wonderful aromas. She picked up a newspaper from a stack at the counter and found a table near the back.

"Can I start you with some sweet tea?" the waitress asked as she laid down a laminated menu and silverware rolled in a paper napkin.

Dorothea drank water with lemon slices at her meals, a habit since her college days. The housemother in her residence cottage had explained that water was important to keep their bodies hydrated and skin refreshed and the touch of citrus aided digestion.

Today, though, change was in order.

"Yes," she said, "I believe I'd like that."

She studied the menu, fascinated by the choices and their names. She supposed the Hungry Farm Boy breakfast might appeal to, well, hungry farm boys but she couldn't imagine eating three eggs, sausage, potatoes, biscuits, gravy and meat all at once. Especially since one of the meat offerings was a breaded steak. Heavens, that was enough for an entire day and the amount of cholesterol was appalling.

31

Dorothea flipped the menu to the other side and studied the dinner choices. The same breaded steak was pictured with a big serving of mashed potatoes and some sort of white sauce over the whole thing. She read the description. Ah, gravy again. The people of this town certainly liked heavy meals.

She spotted a small portion of the menu with more familiar, and sensible, listings. By the time her sweet tea was delivered, she had settled on a meal.

"I'd like the light side salad with chicken," she announced.

"You want that chicken grilled or fried?"

"Uh, grilled."

"House dressing okay?"

Dorothea usually asked for vinaigrette, but she was walking on the wild side today.

"Certainly."

"Crackers or roll?"

"A dinner roll. With authentic butter, please."

"We only got margarine."

Remember where you are.

"That will be fine."

"So we got a light salad with grilled chicken, house dressing and a roll."

"Fried," Dorothea decided with an abrupt change of mind. She was living on the edge, after all. At least for today.

The waitress smiled. "Fried it is. You're gonna like that better anyway."

Dorothea opened the newspaper as she waited. It was a very small edition, nowhere as fat as the Chicago daily normally lying beside Daddy's breakfast plate, with no national news at all. Still she read about the city council's decision to buy new water meters, an upcoming dinner at the Methodist church and how to get a head start on spring planting by forcing bulbs indoors.

She reached the classified section just as her meal arrived.

She continued to read, knowing how appalled Patrice would be if she could see her now. Notices about lost dogs and found horses led to the help wanted section. She would have skipped over those ads entirely if one hadn't jumped out at her, boxed with a bold line around it.

"Advice columnist needed. Must have good grasp of language and grammar boosted by common sense. Apply in person at The Current-Democrat office."

She could do that. Her literary skills were excellent and her courses in women's studies had taught her much about the human condition. If she wasn't just passing through…

Dorothea discreetly studied the other diners as she finished her salad. People of modest means, yes, but mannerly and friendly to those who came and went. She suspected their casual dress was part of their normal lifestyle but they were clean and neat despite shirts proclaiming their love of some bearded duck hunters and certain brands of automobiles. None of them looked like they were hiding from an obnoxious and unwanted fiancé.

She corrected herself. She wasn't hiding. The purpose of this trip was to gain a little breathing room and recover her sense of self.

"All good, honey?" The waitress was back. "We've got some fresh blackberry cobbler if you're in a mood for dessert."

"Oh, no, but thank you anyway." Dorothea supposed the blackberry cobbler, like the delicious sweet tea she had enjoyed, was a regional thing. A scoop of sorbet would have been quite welcome, but she hadn't seen that on the menu.

"Come back tomorrow; the special's country dinner with kraut, wieners, fried potatoes and brown beans." The waitress laid the bill on the table. "Rumor is there's going to be chess pie, too."

Dorothea laid a ten-dollar bill on the table as a tip and tucked the newspaper into her purse. Maybe she could spend the night and go to the newspaper office in the morning. Applying for a job would be good experience. Her father and Patrice might think her only value was as Michael's wife but she was certain she could find employment back in

Chicago. This would be her trial run at being interviewed.

"Is there a hotel nearby?" she asked the middle-aged man who took her money at the cash register. "Perhaps a Hilton?"

He chuckled.

"Afraid not. But my Aunt Louise rents out guest rooms. Let me give her a call."

Dorothea waited while he disappeared behind a swinging door. He returned in mere minutes nodding his head.

"You're in luck. Not only does Aunt Lou have rooms, but the cottage behind her house is also empty." He grabbed a pen and jotted directions on the back of a piece of register tape.

"She's expecting you."

Dorothea walked out of the diner with lightness in her step. She was doing fine on her own. She'd get a good night's sleep, stop by the newspaper in the morning for her first job interview ever and decide what came next. Maybe she'd set the GPS for the scenic route and make her way to Florida. After all, the journey was supposed to be the fulfilling part and not the destination. What could be more adventurous than the back roads of the South?

****

"What do you mean, she's not here?" Anger filled Michael's voice as he glared at Patrice. She answered with a frosty stare.

"Dorothea told the staff she was going out. No one has heard from her since."

"And they let her go? Just like that?"

"She's not a child." Patrice's tone was even and quiet. "Her father spoke to her earlier in the day. Apparently she was interested in spending time at their Florida home to recover from the excitement of your proposal. I'm sure we'll hear from her soon."

"That's not going to help." Michael threw his hands up in frustration. "My parents are expecting us to join them for dinner in twenty minutes. Dorothea's failure to appear is not going to endear her to my mother."

"Simply tell them she's ill."

"More like childish and irresponsible."

One sharp turn and he was gone, heels clicking on the parquet floor of the entry hall. Patrice watched him leave with mixed feelings. She'd never seen this side of the man before. But he was the perfect type of husband for Dorothea—patient, understanding and willing to overlook her inability to deal with real life. She sighed. Victor had spoiled that girl.

She glanced at her watch. He would be home soon. She'd spent most of her day here, at his house, making calls and verifying addresses. Pulling together a proper engagement party in mere weeks was a challenge, but if that's what Victor wanted, her duty was to make it happen.

Patrice pulled her cell phone from her bag and tried Dorothea's number again. And once more, her call went straight to voice mail.

Little brat.

Chapter Three

"You must be the young lady Bruce called about."

The woman, rotund with graying hair and bright eyes, opened the door wide and invited Dorothea to come in. The brick Victorian house had been easy to find. Burning logs crackled in the fireplace to offer a warm welcome. An oriental rug covered solid oak floors; period chairs offered a place to sit and enjoy the ambience. Dorothea instantly felt at home.

"You have a beautiful home," she said. "It's been in the family for over a hundred years. I'm just the current caretaker. When I'm gone, my kids will have to toss a coin to see who lives here next. I'm leaving it to the two of them together, and they know I'll come back and haunt them if it's sold.

"Now let's decide which room best suits you. I think maybe the rose suite. Let's see what you think."

Dorothea followed her hostess through a beautifully appointed sitting room and up a set of stairs with a turn in the middle. They crossed a hallway and into a bedroom with a small parlor with the same cream walls and rose-colored accents.

The décor was charming. Dorothea was pleased to see another fireplace with flames leaping from artificial logs.

"What a lovely room. I'm sure I'll be quite comfortable here."

"Well, good." Lou clapped her hands. "Houses have personalities just like people, and I knew you'd be compatible. Now let me get you some towels. The bathroom's just down the hall, and it's all yours."

Dorothea waited until Lou bustled away to push down on the mattress and pat the pillow. Both were medium firm like hers at home. That was comforting. So was the thick, soft towel she dried off with after her before-bed bath in the claw foot tub. She fell asleep almost instantly and woke to sunshine pouring through the pale pink sheers at the window. She dressed in her new clothes with anticipation and a little trepidation.

Fairy tales had been her favorite books from the time she learned to read. The window seat in the sunroom was a perfect place to curl up and lose herself in a world of castles and magic spells, the inevitable victory of good over evil. Even though her father had called her his little princess, she never felt like one. She still didn't. The ones in story tales were beautiful or charming or feisty, all the things she realized early on she'd never be. They escaped the wiles of witches and wolves while she was protected from the darker side of life.

Being good was the foundation of her life. And good girls didn't sneak into other people's cottages or crash a ball.

Dorothea checked her image in the mirror one last time and fluffed her hair. So she might be a little old to run away from home for the first time. It was still a first step onto the path of disobedience.

The scent of coffee reached her as she went downstairs. Lou waited in the foyer with a tray of muffins, a large bowl of mixed fresh fruit and a carafe of what Dorothea found to be a special blend her hostess ordered off the Internet. The fire was smaller but offered a nice warmth on this chilly morning.

This feels like home.

This could never happen in her father's rarified circle where no one sat down with the cook to share a meal. They were served from menus made up weekly and approved. Patrice took care of that for the Pfister household, but Dorothea always knew in advance what mealtime would bring. Even when they went out, which was often enough, her father usually suggested an entrée.

So this was how the other half lived. She liked it.

"Would it be all right for me to stay a second night?" she asked. "I'll gladly pay in advance if necessary."

"You stay as long as you'd like," Lou said. "You're the quietest guest I've ever had. It feels wrong to even charge you."

"Oh, no," Dorothea insisted. "I must pay."

"I said it didn't feel right," Lou answered with a grin. "I didn't say I wouldn't take your money. Here's what we'll do. You stay as long as you like and give whatever you think is fair when you leave."

"No, no. I can't take advantage of you."

Lou speared a chunk of pineapple onto her plate before replying, "My dear, I can't imagine you ever taking advantage of a single soul."

The compliment warmed Dorothea and made her glad she hadn't gone to the airport. A road trip seemed to be what she needed.

Although the air outside seemed chilly when she left the cozy house for her car, it wasn't cold. No snow covered the ground, and the sun had prewarmed her car's interior. Her good mood continued as she drove back into the heart of the small downtown and found the newspaper office tucked between a consignment store and a beauty parlor. An older lady with obviously fake red hair greeted Dorothea. Once she learned their visitor was inquiring about the advice columnist position, she directed Dorothea to the only walled office.

The door was open, but Dorothea knocked on the doorframe and waited for a "come in" before entering. Based on the stereotype from movies, she expected a gruff man in a wrinkled white shirt, the knot on his tie pulled halfway down. The man behind the desk was maybe forty, wore a T-shirt and jumped up to pull a stack of files off a chair so she could sit down.

"Len Williams. Supposedly the person in charge, although sometimes this place just runs amok. What can I do for you today?"

"I'm interested in the position you have advertised."

"You want to be the next Sally Ann." He made it a statement, not a question. Dorothea nodded.

Len leaned back in his worn chair and studied her.

Dorothea in return studied the man's desk and the items on the wall behind him. A painting of a faded Winn-Dixie grocery building hung beside framed certificates of awards from newspaper association contests. A long Martha White bag was nailed up as well. Dorothea found the quirky addition charming.

"Tell me a little about yourself," Len finally said. "Starting with your name."

"D...Dixie," she said, suddenly remembering the hairdresser's remark about her being a new woman. She grabbed the name from the painting and added "White" from the flour sack.

But what did it matter? It's not as if she was going to be hired. This was just practice.

"From Joliet, Illinois." She began to fabricate a life story for Dixie. "I've been a private tutor for several years, but my students are graduating this year and no longer need me. Since I've always had a yen for warmer climates, I decided it was time to move."

"Pick Cardington from a map, did you?"

"I stopped for dinner last night and then drove around a little. This is a beautiful little town, the sort I've always imagined myself living in."

"The job doesn't pay much."

How much, Dorothea wondered, was that? Not that it mattered, of course.

"I am quite frugal, and I also received a modest inheritance when my grandmother died.

My savings are sufficient to take care of my immediate needs for some time."

"I see." Len fell silent; Dorothea decided she said enough. The simpler she made Dixie's story, the easier it would be to keep it straight.

"Have you written before?"

"I have a bachelor's degree in English with an emphasis on creative writing."

"Creativity is something you need to follow Sally Ann." Dorothea startled when Len abruptly straightened up his chair and leaned toward her. "Tell you what. Take some of these letters home tonight, write the way you'd answer them and come see me tomorrow."

Dorothea walked out with a manila file folder and a promise to be back at ten the next day. This was insane. She should have confessed, explained to the gentleman she was only interviewing for the experience. Then again, he hadn't offered her the position. This bit of writing was part of the application process. Right?

****

"We need to call the police."

"Now, Michael, there's no need to go to extremes." Victor poured a little more bourbon in his glass and topped off his future son-in-law's.

"She's been gone thirty-six hours," Michael retorted. "The police checked the condo in Florida, and she's not there. We both know she's not a good driver. She could be off the road somewhere. Hurt and dying even."

"Dorothea seemed a bit overwhelmed when we sat down together to review the plans." Patrice was drinking tea; it was far too early in the day for a lady to imbibe hard liquor. "I would imagine she is at a friend's house."

"What friend?" Michael retorted. "Has she ever done anything this stupid before?"

"Calm down." Victor's command was sharp. "She has delicate sensibilities like her late mother. Patience is the key."

Michael tossed back his drink and reached for the decanter. Victor hadn't realized the depth of the boy's affection for Dorothea until now. He was distraught but getting soused wouldn't change anything. Victor was worried too. Disappearing like this wasn't like his little girl. He wasn't about to say a word to either Michael or Patrice, but he was anticipating a ransom demand. Or worse. He knew he had enemies.

That's why the police were a bad idea. At this point, there was no reason for Dorothea's absence to become public.

"Stay here," he ordered. "I'll be right back."

Victor moved swiftly down the hall to his study. Unlocking the desk, he found the name and number he was looking for. He had used this particular private detective in the past and found the man to be both dogged and discreet. It couldn't hurt to hire him now.

Victor rejoined the others ten minutes later. Michael was still drinking.

"Although I'm certain there's no reason for concern, I've asked Rick Rahall to do a little work," he announced. "He's done background searches and other work for me in the past and is quite good. I hope this reassures you, Michael."

"I just want her back."

His words slurred slightly which disturbed Victor. One problem at a time. When Dorothea was home, he'd have a talk with Michael about watching his liquor.

"And I want you to hold it together." Victor's words were sharp. "Rahall will be here in an hour or so. Patrice, please tell the kitchen staff to prepare a light lunch before he arrives. I think we can all do with a bite."

The private detective showed up right on time wearing a dark burgundy polo shirt, worn jeans and a baseball cap. He greeted Victor and nodded in turn to Michael and Patrice as he was introduced to each. They met in the study with the door closed to keep the staff from overhearing.

"So that's it in a nutshell, Rahall." Victor gave a heavy sigh. "My last conversation with my little girl was perfectly ordinary. I expected her to be packing when I got home last night. She would never miss a social obligation as important as dinner with the Butterwells."

"Dorothea always does what she's supposed to." Michael cut in. "That's one of the things that made me fall in love with her, the way she understands how life works."

Rick resisted the temptation to deck the bastard. Butterwell was toasted, the smell of bourbon rolling off him. Every word he'd said about the Pfister girl was condescending, as if she were a well-trained sheep dog instead of the woman the guy planned to marry. He knew rich people were different but still.

He intended to check out Butterwell first.

"Could I see her room?" he asked.

"Patrice will take you upstairs." Victor sounded a little shaken. "I didn't see anything out of order."

"Just routine. Seeing where she lives helps me understand her a little."

Rick's own apartment consisted of three rooms, all of them medium messy and furnished with cheap stuff from discount stores. This one bedroom was almost as big as his whole place. White crown molding topped pale green walls. Carpet as soft as deep moss and the same color covered the entire floor. Cream-colored pleated drapes covered window sheers, which matched the heavy comforter on the bed.

The place was hotel room neat. The only personal touches were the framed photos on the glass-topped dressing table. Rick picked them up, studied each in turn. They were all of either the girl and Victor or just Victor alone. Odd that she didn't have a single picture of her with the boyfriend.

He also noticed but didn't examine the obviously expensive ring on the dresser top.

Either she was afraid to wear a rock that size out in public or forgot to put it on when she left. Unless she'd left it behind on purpose, but that didn't make sense. Butterwell had only proposed two days ago.

Rick moved to the bed, pulling open the drawer of the bedside table. It held an address book, a hardback biography of some female astronaut Rick had never heard of and a bottle of saline nasal spray. Nothing unusual there.

There was something odd on the bed.

"Does she normally carry her cell phone?" he asked the woman lingering in the doorway.

"Without question," Patrice replied. "Dorothea is very responsible." "So this isn't hers?" He gestured toward the gray-cased smart phone.

"Oh, dear." Patrice started for the phone; Rick stopped her.

"Please don't touch it." He pulled a plastic glove from his pocket as well as a see-through evidence bag. He jotted the location and date on the bag before he tucked the phone inside. This explained why those calls were going to voice mail.

The clothes hanging in the closet and tucked into her bureau drawers were expensive and conservative. For someone so young, she tended toward dark colors and what his mother used to call *eternals*, clothes that never went out of style. Even the party gowns in their clear bags were dark green, burgundy or black.

Patrice stayed at his elbow to watch every move he made. He was beginning to see how things worked around here. That turned out to be an advantage when the woman was able to print off a computer spreadsheet with the Pfister woman's credit card information along with her Social Security and driver's license numbers. Rick needed to stay on her good side. Patrice knew everything.

He left a few minutes later with a promise to call the second he found anything out.

"Money's no object," Victor said as he handed him a hefty check as a retainer. "Do what you have to. The only thing that matters is my little girl's safety."

The boyfriend didn't even say goodbye. Rick wasn't sure whether he rubbed the guy the wrong way or if the dude was too drunk to speak. Not that it was any skin off his nose. He long ago learned to keep his out of other people's business.

****

Only a few people were in the diner when Dorothea stopped in for an early lunch. She was ravenous. She supposed the condition came from a combination of stress and the excitement of doing something unplanned and inappropriate for the first time in her life. Patrice would be appalled to know

Dorothea was about to immerse herself in other people's personal problems. Her father, no doubt, would pat her on the head and tell her she wasn't worldly enough to give anyone advice.

How many times had he smiled at her and said, "You don't know how the world works, honey, and I'm glad of that. I love you just the way you are."

Which, according to what she overheard Michael say at the country club, was that she was best suited to be a brood cow with the intelligence of one. The memory of his stupid proposal and how she had to accept it fired her determination to ace the rest of this job interview.

Although, she reminded herself, she couldn't accept the job. She had to go home eventually. Or to Florida where her father believed her to be now. She supposed letting him know her change in plans would be the correct thing to do.

She was so tired of doing the expected thing.

"Hi again." The same woman who had served her the previous night handed her a menu and laid down the napkin-wrapped silverware. "Decided to stay a while, did you?"

"Another day or so." Dorothea handed back the menu and waved toward the white board hanging on the wall. "I'd like the meatloaf special."

"Mashed potatoes with gravy, green beans okay?"

"That will be fine. Oh, and I'd like a glass of sweet tea as well."

"You got it."

Dorothea reviewed her time with Len as she waited for her meal to arrive. He seemed like a very nice man even though he did have a messy office. She wondered idly if there was no cleaning service or if he preferred not to have his things touched. Some people were like that.

She wished she knew more about the mysterious Sally Ann, the retiring advice columnist. Did she have a sharp wit, or were her answers serious? Was her grammar perfect, or did she adopt a breezy tone?

Stop it!

The editor wasn't looking for a clone. He was interested in her skills as a writer.

The small restaurant began to fill as she enjoyed her meal. She watched people come and go. Some were laborers judging by their clothing while others wore professional attire. This was a small town. Dorothea wondered how they earned their livings, what their days were like the rest of the time.

A small wave of guilt washed over her. She never thought about such things before, but merely taken for granted everything that didn't directly affect her.

Leaving the diner, she drove through the few blocks of downtown looking for an office goods store. There didn't seem to be any. She parked in front of the modest post office and walked inside.

"End of the street, turn left and go two blocks," the clerk directed. "The place is called Charley's This and That. He sells a little of everything."

The description was accurate. Dorothea wandered up and down the aisles of the long building, amazed at the variety of items piled high on tables and covering shelves. Brown cloth gloves nestled against cast iron skillets and cans of dog food. She eventually found an assortment of wire-bound notebooks and selected a fat one with narrow rules. On her way toward the old fashioned cash register by the door, she spotted a glass-fronted case holding electronic equipment.

"Gently used and guaranteed for thirty days," read a hand-lettered sign taped to the front. Dorothea stopped and studied the items, her attention caught by a laptop. And it was only a hundred dollars. How in the world could this man make money with prices like this?

"I'd like that computer," she said to the man she assumed was Charley.

"Need a printer? Got one for ten bucks that works good."

Dorothea stopped herself from correcting his grammar to change that good to well. The man was an entrepreneur, not an English professor. The price was remarkable enough for her to overlook such a small matter. She pulled two hundred dollar bills from her purse.

"Honey, I can't cash a bill that big," Charley said. "You're my first customer of the day. I can take a credit card if you have one or you can run down to the bank and have them break it."

Since she didn't know where the bank was located, Dorothea chose the first option. She watched as he plugged a small square of plastic into his cell phone, swiped her card and handed it back. That was certainly different. But effective, since her purchase went through with no problem.

She walked out carrying the box in which he'd put her purchases with a sense of satisfaction. She wished Michael could see her now. Patrice too. Who needed a designer and a staff when she had a good brain to use?

Lou's enthusiastic response buoyed her new self-confidence.

"If you got this from Charley, you got a good one." Lou hooked up the computer and printer. Dorothea watched so she could do it the next time. "Probably got new ink in there, too. He doesn't sell anything he wouldn't use himself."

She sat down on the bed and watched as Dorothea acquainted herself with the keyboard and commands.

"Does this mean you're hired?" she asked.

"Not yet." Dorothea abandoned the computer and turned to her new friend. "He wants me to create some sample columns so he can see my writing. I hope I'm able to do it."

"Why couldn't you?"

Dorothea pondered Lou's question. Her writing skills were excellent. She had a logical mind, and she was an organized person. She wasn't sure those pluses would cancel out her one big negative.

"I'm not the kind of person people come to with their problems," she admitted. "My friends don't call me for advice or seek me out when they're feeling blue. I'm the one they invite when they have an extra theater ticket. Maybe I'm too superficial to do this."

"No more of that talk." Lou slapped her hand against the mattress. "You had the gumption to apply for the job, and besides, Len is a good judge of character. He wouldn't be interested in you if he had any doubts."

Lou's support warmed Dorothea and gave her courage. She'd do her best; that was all she could do. Either the editor would like it or he wouldn't.

"I'm going to let you get to work now," Lou said. "You have any problems with that thing, holler. I used all kinds of computers when I worked at the high school. They're just machines. Remember that."

The help button became Dorothea's ally as she acquainted herself with the word processing program. When she decided she knew enough to create a file and print it, she closed the laptop and opened the file of letters Len had sent with her. She took a big breath and let it out. Time to prove herself.

****

The key to being a good investigator, Rick had long ago learned, was knowing the right people. That and being able to navigate the Internet. He put off making calls until he did a little on-line research about the missing woman. Could be that her family's perception of dear little Dorothea didn't match reality. Just because her father and fiancé thought she was at a charity planning committee didn't mean she really was. She might have friends in low places or some not-so-savory boyfriend they knew nothing about.

An hour later, he was willing to concede her family was right. Dorothea Pfister didn't even have a social media account. There were no pictures of her drunk in a club, half-naked at the beach or cozying up to tattooed guy. What he did find were newspaper articles and newsletter blurbs confirming what the family told him.

She was most definitely a good girl. And good girls didn't disappear like she had. Time to make calls.

Patrice had jotted down the information about the two credit cards to which Dorothea had access. He called the companies; there had been no use of either one in the last two days.

An old acquaintance in the state police agreed to send out information on Dorothea's car and checked the statewide computer system for any accidents involving a Saab like the one she was driving. Again, Rick came up empty.

This might be harder than he thought.

Facing nothing but dead ends started him looking at the other principals, mainly Michael Butterwell. Something about the guy didn't sit right. Maybe it was because he was sloshed by noon. But maybe it was because he didn't seem to know much about the habits of the woman he supposedly was head over heels for.

Rick's trip into cyberspace this time garnered a wealth of information. Butterwell wasn't hesitant about his presence there. He tweeted, posted and loved to put up pictures of himself. He also came across to Rick as intelligent but shallow, the kind of man who'd cut corners to get what he wanted.

And use someone like Dorothea without a second thought.

Rick leaned back in his well-worn office chair and studied the pictures he'd borrowed. Dorothea looked like she came from an earlier era with that severe hairstyle and librarian style of clothing. Maybe that's how people from her social stratification dressed, though. He didn't move in those rarified circles. Nor did he have any desire to.

Sighing, he set aside the search for Dorothea. He checked the mail, wrote a check for the electric bill that was on disconnect and printed out an invoice for the last job he finished. But she was on his mind as he headed out the door for a hot bologna sandwich and a cup of the best coffee in town at the bar down the street.

Rick came back to find the phone's message light blinking. He wasn't surprised to hear Victor's voice asking if he'd made any progress yet. He returned the call. Patrice answered.

He realized within seconds that Victor was the only one worried.

"If she was ten years younger, I'd chalk it up to teen rebellion," Patrice said. "Her father has given her everything, and she's never appreciated it. If he hadn't been so involved with her life, Dorothea would have gone to some university where partying trumped academics.

Endowing a chair at the college of his choice was a good move on his part."

"Oh?" Rick knew doing something like that cost a pretty penny.

"The administration was very cooperative in keeping Dorothea safe."

Rick was pretty sure she meant *coddled*.

"From what I've learned about her, she seems to have a pretty good head on her shoulders. I can't imagine her going wild."

"Thanks to her father. And my influence, of course. I've continued with the wedding planning despite her absence. One can't simply book the right caterer at the last minute. The florist suggests exotic flowers at the reception, and here we are, unable to consult Dorothea on anything."

"I'm doing my best to find her," he said.

"Oh, I know, and we are so grateful. Have you spoken to her college roommate? Althea something? She used to speak of going to Mexico to study the Inca ruins with her."

At the end of their conversation, Rick knew one thing: The woman resented Dorothea.

Her final remark made it clear.

"She simply wants attention," Patrice pronounced. "She'll call her father when she's tired of playing hooky, and he'll hurry to her as always."

Rick figured it was the other way around: Patrice was the attention-seeker. Not that it was any of his business. He made it a practice not to get personally involved with a case. That could only lead to trouble.

Chapter Four

I love my children, I really do. But am I being unreasonable to expect them to call before coming to my house? My son brought his new girlfriend to meet me and I was in the bathtub when they walked in! Any suggestions on how to gently remind them I am entitled to a life of my own?
Rebellious Mom

Dorothea understood this woman's dilemma. She hadn't realized until this mini-vacation how precious little choice she had in how her life played out. Growing up, her bedroom was only a place for sleeping instead of the kind of retreat she might have liked. When her father was in, she kept him company unless he was too involved with work he brought home. And when he was out, Dorothea spent her time with charity work or similar enterprises approved of and organized by Patrice.

She reread the letter and then started typing.

Dear Rebellious Mom:
It's time to roll up the welcome mat and cut the cord! Installing new locks—and using them—

would get the message across. But you may want to try a gentler approach first. Talk to your children and explain that just as you respect their privacy, you'd like them to appreciate your need for advance notice. If that doesn't work, there are lots of locksmiths listed in the phone book!

Dixie

Dorothea ran a spell check, read the answer again and hit the save key. One down. Len had asked for five or six answers, which she assumed would be a column's worth. She picked up the next from the pile.

My neighbors are great and used to be the best in the world. That's until they got a cat. They'd still be the best if they kept Princess indoors. But they let her out every day "just for air" and she hightails it to my flower bed which she has decided is her litter box. She also sits on top of the air-conditioning unit to tease my dog through the window. Help! I just want things to be the way they used to be.

Fed Up Next Door

Ooh, this one was hard. Dorothea never had a pet. Her father believed animals belonged on a farm, and even fish should stay in the ocean. She set the letter aside. This needed research.

She'd have to answer it in the next column.

She caught herself. There would be no next column. This was an *experience*, not a real job interview. Tomorrow morning, afternoon at the latest, she'd be driving out of town forever.

The next letter was definitely in her bailiwick.

My best friend is getting married in a couple of months and I'd love to take my boyfriend with me as my guest. He's perfect except for one thing. His table manners leave a lot to be desired. Should I invite him and hope everyone can overlook his deficiency? I'm afraid he'll take it badly if I tell him he's eating all wrong.
Always a Bridesmaid

Dorothea had been drilled on etiquette since she was old enough to hold a spoon. Some of the girls at boarding school had the same problem as this writer's beau.

Dear Always A Bridesmaid:
If he's perfect in every other way, you better hang onto this one! Invite him to dinner and set your table for a formal meal. Suggest that your own table manners are rusty and ask him to watch you to make sure you don't make a mistake. Watching you may help him improve his own without hurting his

feelings. Or you can spare his feelings and leave him at home. Or, plan B, take him along and supply a big trough.

    Dixie

      Dorothea's shoulders ached from working with the unfamiliar keyboard at the dressing table in her room. She needed a break before she edited her work. Standing up, she stretched one way and then the other. Maybe a brisk walk was called for.

      "Knock, knock." Lou spoke from just outside the open bedroom door.

      "Oh, hello. Come on in."

      "I don't want to disturb you. I made cranberry orange muffins and thought you might want to join me in a taste test."

      "I'd like that very much."

      They settled at the small drop-leaf table in the cheery kitchen. The scent of the muffins mixed with the smell of brewing coffee, an aroma that held great appeal for Dorothea. Again she marveled at how a house this big, with such large rooms and high ceilings, could feel so cozy. Her own certainly didn't. Then again, she rarely entered the kitchen except to ask about the week's menu.

      Lou carried the conversation, filling Dorothea in on the small town news of Cardington.

      So what if she didn't know the people? Listening to Lou was nice, especially since there were no "And, remember, Dorothea…" or "Make sure you check your calendar," which her conversations with Patrice often included.

"Just listen to me, taking up your time." Lou shook her head and stood, gathering their used cups and plates. "A young girl like you has better things to do."

That remark started Dorothea wondering what other women her age did here in this small town. Back in her room, she flipped through the pages of the newspaper hoping she could find a clue.

New year, new you! The words jumped out from a colorful ad for a local dance studio, which seemed to offer more than just dance. The schedule showed a yoga session three days a week. This was one of those days. But she didn't have yoga clothing.

No. Dorothea would let that matter. But Dixie, advice columnist extraordinaire, wouldn't care. She rummaged through the Walmart bag and pulled out a pair of soft pants and colorful knit top she'd purchased. They'd do.

She changed quickly before she lost her courage. Finding Lou in front of the television set in a small room off the foyer, she explained where she was going and that she'd be back later.

"Oh, that's Amy's class," Lou said. "You'll love her. Hold on a minute. I'll send a couple of muffins for her."

Once she accepted the small bag, Dorothea knew it was too late to chicken out. The day was mild so she set out walking. According to Lou, the studio was only a couple of blocks away.

About a dozen women were laying out mats and chattering when Dorothea walked in. A thirty-something brunette came over, introducing herself as Amy.

"These are for you." Dorothea handed her the muffins. "Lou sent them."

"Ooh, yummy." Amy peeked inside the bag. "She is such a good cook."

A few moments later, Dorothea was standing beside a mat borrowed from Amy and ready for this new adventure. An hour later, after stretching and moving, she realized either yoga was more demanding than she had believed or she was out of shape. Or maybe both.

"You did great." Amy rewarded her with a quick, surprising hug. "Come back Friday, okay? And tell Lou thanks for me."

Dorothea called out as she walked back into the house but no one answered her hello. She took a quick shower and realized she was hungry. She dressed, started the car and headed for the diner. The white board announced the evening special as baked chicken with dressing and two sides. The dessert of the day was apple crisp with ice cream.

Oh, she was tempted. But the afternoon's session reminded her to be mindful so she ordered a cup of vegetable soup and a salad with light ranch dressing. She did give in and order sweet tea. She had absolutely fallen in love with its wonderful taste.

Once again, a fire blazed in the entry hall and a tray sat near it, topped with a tray of baked goods and a coffee carafe. The luscious frosted brownies were hard to resist. When Lou came in the room, Dorothea was curled up watching the fire, with her half-eaten brownie. She passed along Amy's thanks and offered a quick recap of the yoga session when prompted.

That night, Dorothea slept the best she had in a long time. She had a history of restless sleep—but she didn't wake even once. She was in a great mood as she dressed, fluffed up her hair and went to visit Len again.

"Love it." Len looked up from the printed pages and grinned. "Like I said, the job doesn't pay much. You can drop in once a week and pick up the letters if you want to work from home.

Or if you'd rather, I can clear off a desk for you."

Work from home? That was an option?

Excitement filled her. She could take the position, ask for the letters to be mailed to her and e-mail her column to Len. She would love to throw

Michael's ring back at him while telling him she was good for something besides boosting his career.

"If this is a formal employment offer, I accept."

"Great! Now let's talk about how we're going to introduce you to our readers. Stella— that's her at the desk out front—had a great idea. Since it's almost Valentine's Day, she thought we could have a contest. Win a Date with Dixie. You are single, right?"

"Yes." She dragged out the syllable. What in the world was the man suggesting?

"We'll run your picture and a little piece about you in this week's paper. And we'll ask our readers to nominate single men to go on a date with you. That will make a great little story, and we'll give each of the guys a year's subscription to the paper and a gas gift card. How does that sound to you?"

Horrible. Frightening. Insane.

"Interesting," she finally replied.

"Stella knows everybody in town, so she'll screen the nominees. Of course, there will be ground rules to ensure each of them treats you like a lady. Glad you're a good sport with it."

Len stood and offered his hand.

"Welcome aboard," he said as Dorothea shook it. "This town is going to fall in love with you."

****

"Are you totally incompetent or just not trying?"

Rick looked up from his desk at the man who stormed in without knocking.

"Hello, Butterwell." He looked up, nodded and went back to checking his e-mail.

"I'm talking to you, jackass." Michael planted both hands on the edge of the desk and leaned in. Rick caught the aroma of whiskey. "It's been four days. Where's Dorothea?"

"If I knew, you'd know."

Rick kept his tone even. He had plenty of experience in dealing with angry clients.

"Victor will pay if you want more money. He'll do whatever it takes to find her."

"So will I," Rick snapped. "She's not in a hospital around here, no one's spotted her car, and I figure if her father had received a ransom demand, I'd know. She's a grown woman. She can take a vacation without answering to you."

"I don't like your attitude!"

"I don't like drunks yelling at me. I suggest you leave."

He half-expected Michael to come across the desk at him. Instead, his unwelcome visitor turned and stomped out. Rick was more than happy to see him go. He didn't need a reminder that things weren't going well.

He closed his e-mail and picked up the phone. Time for his daily calls on this wild-goose chase. He started with airport security to see if her car had turned up there. A half hour later, he was as frustrated as he had been before he started.

He flipped open a manila folder and stared at Dorothea's photo for the hundredth time. Where was she? He was surprised the press hadn't gotten wind of her absence, but then again, if she was as private as her family claimed, he shouldn't be.

Despite Butterwell's game face, the man seemed more concerned about himself than about his missing girlfriend. Rick had plenty of experience with distraught boyfriends and husbands. Butterwell's behavior came off more like an act. The uncharitable thought crossed his mind that the opportunity to latch onto Victor's money might be what be what Butterwell was grieving over.

The phone rang; he grabbed it as soon as he saw the caller ID. One of his contacts at the credit card companies had come through. He hoped.

"Thanks for the info. Let me know if anything else shows up, okay?"

This looked like a dead end, but it was at least something. The chances that a rich girl would make a minimal purchase at a place called Charley's This and That in some nothing town in Kentucky were slim to none. He'd bet his back teeth the card had been stolen. As so often happened, his one chase had branched into two. Finding who possessed the credit card now didn't mean he'd find Dorothea. But it was a start.

He debated calling Victor, at last deciding it was too soon in the investigation. Once he verified the card was indeed in the hands of someone else, he'd make that call. Normally he'd check with law enforcement, too. But Victor had been adamant about not calling the police.

He hit the computer and searched for Cardington, Kentucky. The place turned out to be barely a blip on the map. Population just over three thousand with no industry to speak of.

He searched for the store that ran the credit card. The place didn't have a website or even a Facebook page. Probably a pawnshop with spotty records. He'd dealt with that before.

Rick clicked back onto the map of Cardington he pulled up before and widened the view. The place really was in the middle of nowhere. The interstate running past it looked like its only distinguishing feature. Definitely not where Dorothea Pfister would feel at home.

Damn. He had a road trip on his hands.

****

"What more can you do, Victor?" Patrice laid her hand on his arm and looked into his worried eyes. "You have to relax and trust the investigator. If Dorothea had come to harm, we'd know by now."

"It's been almost a week and not a word."

"Five days," Patrice corrected. "She's probably with a friend and doesn't realize you're concerned."

"Concerned? That's putting it lightly. I'm scared to death, Patty. She could be hurt or dead. Or even worse."

"We talked a bit on the way home from the club the night Michael proposed. I think she's overwhelmed and needs time to adjust. Quite honestly, I'm not sure she ever expected to marry."

"I hope you're right." Victor sighed and leaned forward to bury his head in his hands. "I just want her home."

"Let me get you a drink. That will help you relax."

Patrice rose from the leather couch in his study and walked over to the bar tucked away in the corner. She was so sick of hearing Dorothea's name. The little snip was probably shut up in a hotel room. Curled in a ball in the middle of a bed, no doubt, overcome by her deficiencies. Michael's proposal was supposed to solve things, not complicate them. As soon as Dorothea was out of this house and into one on the other side of town, nothing would stand in the way of her own plans with Victor. She'd given the best years of her life to him. She wanted that ring on her hand soon.

She ran her fingers across his shoulders as she handed him a stiff highball. They'd practically gone into mourning these last few days. She was so ready for a night at the country club with his friends. Spending night after night listening to him fret was so depressing.

"Maybe I should give Rahall a call."

"Victor, it's after eight," Patrice protested. "Wait until morning. The man is entitled to a little personal time, you know."

"You're right." Victor offered her a wan smile as he took her hand. "What would I do without you?"

"Don't worry. You'll never have to."

Triumph filled her. Maybe this silly disappearing act of Dorothea's offered an advantage after all.

Chapter Five

Dorothea's conscience bothered her. She'd agreed to Len's marketing plan even though it meant extending her stay. She didn't mind missing dinner with Michael's parents at all, but her father would worry if he discovered she wasn't in Florida. Yet calling him could lead to questions she didn't want to answer, and Patrice checked all her father's e-mail.

A note would be appropriate. Stopping by Charley's This and That, she purchased a box of stationery for a ridiculously low price. She composed her missive over a glass of sweet tea at the diner, settling for short and simple.

Dear Daddy,

I've decided to make my travel to Florida more leisurely than a plane flight and am driving down. I'll give you a call when I arrive, perhaps in a week or two. I am so appreciating the chance to see new things. Don't worry; I'm great!

Love,
Dorothea

The message was vague but reassuring, she decided as she slipped the folded paper into a matching envelope and addressed it to her father at his office. Looking through her wallet, she found a stamp. Now all she needed was a mailbox. Lou would know where to find one.

She found her hostess putting on her jacket when she arrived back at the bed and breakfast.

"I'm off to the store if you'd like to ride along," Lou offered. "I thought you might like a chance to get out of Cardington for a little while."

"I'd love that. Are you going to the Walmart by any chance?"

Lou laughed. "Just the supermarket. Although I could swing by if you need something."

"Oh, no no." Dorothea certainly didn't want to take her out of her way. "After all, I'm only looking."

The supermarket wasn't what Dorothea expected. This was nothing like the organic food store she occasionally frequented. She accompanied Lou up and down the aisles, content to look rather than shop although she did pick up a bag of grapes, a box of granola bars and almond milk.

"I take it you're planning to stay a little longer," Lou remarked as they waited in the checkout line.

"Another week or two."

"You might like to move into the cottage. It's quite cozy, and you'll have more room." She smiled. "Even a real desk."

A bit more space would be nice, but having a proper place to write was the deciding factor. Dorothea imagined setting up a pencil cup, desk calendar and coaster for her cup. With the right accessories, she could have a mini-office. And wouldn't that shock Michael.

And Patrice. That remark of hers from the night of the party still rankled.

Most *young men these days want a wife with skills of her own.*

Len recognized her skill. He smiled when he read what she'd written. He was willing to pay for her work. When she walked back into Daddy's house with a paycheck and copies of the newspaper, Patrice would have to take back her words. Dorothea would be a success.

Was a success, she reminded herself. The good people of Cardington would be reading her first column on Thursday. Too bad her father didn't subscribe.

No, actually, it was a good thing. If Daddy knew she was here instead of in Florida, he'd send a driver to snatch her up and take her back to Chicago. She wasn't ready to go yet.

"I believe I'd like that," she finally answered Lou.

She was excited at having her own place, even if for a tiny time. For the first time in her life, she'd be living all alone.

Moving from the room to the cottage took four minutes, the length of time she needed to carry her things out the kitchen door and into her new residence. It was as charming as Lou had described. A small bedroom opened off the living area, which had a galley kitchen at the back. A palette of pastels colored the rooms. The effect was soothing and old-fashioned.

Dorothea was relieved to see a full-sized tub in the small bathroom. She wanted to soak in a froth of bubbles before she settled down for what she hoped would be another wonderful night's sleep.

The promised desk sat near a window. Dorothea placed her laptop square in the middle and set up the printer to one side. Her pens were stacked atop the notebooks she'd bought from Charley. She pulled out the center drawer and tucked a few things inside before she ran out to the Saab to retrieve her phone. When she couldn't find it in the center console, she checked under her seat. A thorough search of the whole interior revealed nothing but a paper clip and a half roll of breath mints.

She blew out an exasperated breath. It must have dropped out on one of her stops. At least no one knew, especially not Patrice. The woman would be thrilled to point out one more of her flaws.

Making a mental note to buy one of those disposable ones she'd seen at the supermarket, she hurried out of the cold and into the warmth of the cottage.

Dorothea finally noticed the television in the corner. She stood in the middle of the room, torn between tuning in a news channel to find out what was happening in the world and starting work on her next column. The pile of letters won. She wasn't sure she wanted whatever was happening elsewhere to intrude on her new, albeit temporary life. Fairy tale princesses didn't know a thing about the European financial markets.

A light knock on the door interrupted her as she contemplated how one might respond to an exasperated teenager whose brother hogged the shower and hid her make-up. She opened the door to find Lou standing there with a basket of quick breads and little bag of cheese cubes.

"A housewarming gift." Lou smiled widely. "I thought you might like something to snack on besides your grapes."

"How thoughtful." Lou's culinary talent once more amazed Dorothea. Maybe she could take lessons before she left.

"I'd also like to invite you for dinner. Chicken and dumplings is on the menu because I love them, and there is no way to make only enough for one."

She wasn't about to decline the invitation. An hour later, Dorothea was sitting in the dining room at Lou's looking at a veritable feast of comfort foods. Along with the main dish, Lou had prepared mashed potatoes topped with butter, green beans with onion and bacon, and cornbread she'd baked in a cast iron skillet. Dorothea realized after a few bites this might be one of the most delicious meals she'd ever had. Bad for her health, she was sure, but wonderful.

As they enjoyed lemon pie and coffee by the fire, Dorothea told Lou about the marketing promotion.

"You can trust Stella if she has final approval," Lou said. "Her instincts are right on. Besides, in a town this small everyone knows everyone else. I wonder who they'll be." She shrugged her shoulders. "Well, I guess we'll know in a few days."

****

Two days after that tip from the credit card company, Rick was finally able to hit the road. He'd stuck around Chicago for a reason. A call from a regular client asking for a background on a potential employee was a chance to make good money fast. That was something he wasn't about to turn down for a thin lead on the Pfister woman.

He grabbed a duffel bag and threw in clothes for a couple of days. His phone rang; he answered as he walked out the door.

"Victor Pfister here," he heard. "I need you to stop by the house as soon as possible. I've heard from Dorothea."

****

Rick sat in a chair across the desk from his client and read the brief note. Twice. He'd give her this: she managed say nothing with great elegance.

"Do you have a reason not to believe that she's taking the long way south?" he asked.

"That's totally out of her nature," Victor said.

"She wouldn't do something like that." Michael jiggled the ice cubes in his glass as he answered. "Dorothea can't even get to the club by herself."

"Enough!" Victor's voice was sharp. "We're aware of her shortcomings. Why don't you make yourself another drink and let us talk?"

Here was another scenario with which Rick was all too familiar. Stress brought out the best in some people and the worst in others. He wondered how long Butterwell would stay at the law firm once Victor's daughter was home. That she would return was a given. There was nothing in her note to indicate forcible authorship, and the lack of a ransom demand pretty much ensured she hadn't been taken against her will.

He was gaining a new respect for Dorothea. Considering the other players in this family drama, she might prove the sanest one of all by skipping town.

"What's the postmark on this?" he asked.

"Tennessee. Nashville."

Which would be on the route from Chicago to Florida, Rick realized. As soon as he got out of here, he'd have to see how far Cardington was from the Music City. If someone stole the Pfister woman's purse when she made a gas stop, he had his explanation for that credit card charge. He almost told Victor about the transaction. He probably would have if Butterwell hadn't been there. The less that guy knew, the better.

"I'll head that way and see what I can find," he offered.

"Excellent idea." Victor fiddled with a desk drawer before extending a fat stack of money to Rick. "This should take care of expenses. If it's not enough, add it to your bill."

"Will do." The man really was worried. There had to be a couple of thousand there.

"Keep receipts." Michael issued a curt order. "If you don't, that's going against your pay."

Victor glared at his future son-in-law but kept his mouth shut. Rick decided it was a good time to leave. He promised to call as soon as he knew something and in twenty-four hours even if he didn't. He wasn't surprised to see Butterwell fixing another drink as he left. When he found Dorothea— and he had no doubt he would—he intended to offer a little advice about the foolishness of marrying a drunk.

****

"Here are the top contenders." Len fanned the pictures across what passed for a conference table at the back of the newspaper office. "Stella has given her seal of approval, by the way."

Dorothea studied the seven men in whose company she'd spend her evenings. They all appeared to be about her age. None of them was extraordinarily handsome; none was unusually unattractive. Nor did any remind her of the man waiting for her back home, thank goodness.

"Tell me again how this will work," she said.

"You'll go out with a different one seven nights in a row. Stella will call and tell them they've been chosen and okay their plans. All dates will take place in public places and last about two hours. It's up to you whether you'd like them to pick you up or prefer to meet them at the destination."

Dorothea hadn't been on that many dates in her life. Of course, she wouldn't be going on these. Dixie would. A woman like Dixie wouldn't be afraid to get in a car with any of these gentlemen. After all, Stella knew them and approved.

"They can pick me up at Louise's house." That would be better than letting the men know she was staying alone in the cottage. Besides Lou had already stated her intention of staying up each evening until Dorothea was safely home.

"Sounds like a plan. I'll call lucky number one and let him know he's on for tomorrow night." He gathered up the photos and tucked them in an envelope with several folded pieces of paper. "Stella's put together a bio of each one for you."

Dorothea managed not to let her enthusiasm show as she told Len goodbye and stopped by Stella's desk to thank her for her work. She not only had one date, she had seven of them, a gift from out of the blue. She had a valuable chance to learn about men. Six months with Michael had shown her what she didn't want. This week might reveal what she did.

She dropped by the diner where she was greeted as a regular. She had developed a serious addiction to the fruit cobbler. Today's variety was peach. A man she'd never seen before was sitting at her regular table with a bowl of the ice cream-topped delight when she walked in.

Dorothea picked the next table over. Sweet tea and cobbler appeared without her ordering. She was just too darned predictable when the waitress knew what she'd choose.

"This stuff is fantastic." The stranger held up a fat spoonful and smiled.

"You should try the sweet tea." Dorothea picked up her glass in a similar salute. "They go together well."

"I think I will." He pushed back his coffee cup and motioned for the waitress. "I'd never turn down advice from a beautiful lady."

"You, sir, are a flatterer."

Dorothea took a bite of her cobbler, turning her attention to her food rather than the man beside her. She was pretty sure he was flirting with her. Her confidence was up, but she wasn't ready to flirt back.

Yet. All those upcoming dates might change that.

****

Rick watched the woman from the corner of his eye as he ate. She wasn't a Kentucky native. She had a Midwest accent, her words faster and flatter than the others he'd met here in Cardington. If she looked like a librarian, he might suspect he'd found Dorothea. She had the same oval shaped face, was about the same height and had the same slim body. Her clothes, though, weren't the designer outfits Dorothea's father said she wore, and her hair was shorter, lighter and swung when she moved her head.

She could, however, be a credit card thief.

"I'm looking for a motel," he said. "Can you recommend one?"

The woman smiled. "Nashville's about sixty miles south. That's probably the nearest."

"There's not one here in town?"

"I can recommend a marvelous bed and breakfast. It's a couple blocks from here."

"That would be great."

He jotted down the address and directions. If Nashville was that near, he could run down tomorrow, do some sleuthing and be back here by dinnertime. He opened the newspaper he grabbed off a stack at the counter and flipped through the pages. He stopped his scanning when her face stared up at him from an inside page.

Her name was Dixie White, she was the new advice columnist and about to embark on a series of blind dates. He ripped out the ad and tucked it in his pocket. Funny how her arrival in town coincided with Dorothea's credit card usage. Or maybe not so odd after all.

Rick waited until she left to pay his own bill and drive away. Following Dixie's directions, he found the bed and breakfast without trouble. Fifteen minutes later, he was officially a guest. His hostess Lou offered a slice of lemon cake and fresh coffee.

"If there's anything you need during your stay, be sure to tell me," Lou said as she refilled her cup.

"I think I'll be quite comfortable. My room is very nice."

The upstairs room had a bay window and a view of the side street. His temporary abode was decorated in masculine style with a large navy rug covering the hardwood floor beside the wide bed, matching curtains that kept out the illumination from the streetlight and heavy oak furniture. It was nothing like his own apartment.

"There is only one other guest at the moment, and she's taken the cottage behind the house," Lou added. "You'll meet her soon. Dixie has just gone to work for the local newspaper."

Rick didn't believe in coincidences. Things happened for a reason. In this case, so he could keep an eye on Miss Dixie White.

"Does the whole town usually find dates for newcomers?" he asked. "Not that I'm looking for an order form."

"Oh, no." Lou laughed. "That's just a promotional gimmick."

Rick listened as she explained the concept. Too bad he hadn't arrived in time to apply. But since they were living in virtually the same house, he should have ample time to get acquainted with the woman who might turn out to be a fraud. A friendly one, yes, but still a criminal.

"That's quite an idea," he commented after she finished. "Does it start soon?"

"Tonight. That way all the dates will be over before the Valentine's dance down at the school. The men will be guests of honor. I suppose the idea is that the single women around here will show up to vie for their attention."

"What if Dixie wants one of them for herself?" Lou just smiled.

A log shifted in the fireplace, throwing sparks. When Lou jumped up to tend to it, Rick also stood. The time had come to visit Charley's This and That. Maybe he'd find some great bargains.

The shop was easy to find. Then again, in a town as small as Cardington, everything was easy to find. Rick drove past the elementary school that served as a hub for community activities in after-school hours and three churches of varying denominations. A dollar store, that looked to be brand new, was on the edge of the business district—a loose term for the collection of stores and shops. He took particular notice of the newspaper office.

Charley's turned out to be what Rick's dad always called a junk shop. The name was appropriate because it did indeed hold a little of this and a bit of that. He forgot the purpose of his visit for a time as he wandered through the various displays. This guy had things he hadn't thought of for years, from licorice bull's-eye candy to the scented bars of soap his grandmother used. He picked up a few things on his way to the electronics display where he feigned an interest in a used police scanner.

"Wanna see anything, just let me know." Charley spoke without getting up from his chair. He held a thick mug in his right hand; a newspaper lay folded on his lap.

"Will do."

Dorothea wouldn't be caught dead in a place like this. Rick had dealt with enough wealthy people to know that much. She'd probably break out in hives and swoon at the very idea of using something bought secondhand. If she'd even lower herself to walk in the door of a place like this.

He'd get up early tomorrow and head towards Nashville, her most likely hiding spot. Despite her father's fears, Rick was sure she was whole and hearty on the VIP floor of one of the city's best hotels. A stern suggestion that she get hold of her father and his own call to Victor would wind up this case. He might get even back home in time for the monthly poker session his buddy hosted.

Chapter Six

She definitely needed more clothes. Dorothea could barely stand to look at the boring things she'd brought from her bedroom back home. Dixie would never wear all those dark colors or staid, old lady blouses. She loved color and style. But Cardington wasn't exactly fashion central.

The day was mild for the first of February, so she was glad to be able to walk instead of driving. Lou's treats were too tasty to resist, but Dorothea knew she had to either quit eating them or exercise more. She opted for the latter.

She was on her way to the paper to drop off her column, which was tucked safely inside her purse. Passing the door to the consignment shop, she went in to see what that was all about. And stopped short at the display of bright red clothing by the checkout area.

Dixie would wear red, especially on all these pre-Valentine's dates. She checked a price tag. How could anything be so cheap?

"Try on anything you'd like," said the owner who seemed to pop out of nowhere. "We have some adorable sweaters that just came in."

Dorothea left the store with the promise to come right back to pick up the two bags of clothes she wound up buying. She even found the cutest boots in just her size that looked brand new and some pants and oversized shirts. She wondered why she hadn't discovered the joy of shopping before.

Her elation must have shown because Stella greeted her with "Well, you're in a great mood today," when she walked into the newspaper office.

Dorothea explained where she'd been, which sent Stella down a path of describing every purchase she'd ever made there. Len rescued her, coming through the door with a big smile on his face.

"Just who I wanted to see." He motioned for her to follow him to his desk. "We've got sponsors for all the dates, and the schedule is set. I think our readers are going to love this. And you."

She left with a schedule spit out by a rickety printer detailing when she'd be with who and their destinations as well as a cell phone Len produced from a drawer.

"The phone store down the street trades usage for advertising," he explained when Dorothea protested. "I'll be popping in during each date to take a photo for the paper and to put up at the party. This way I can let you know if I have to go to an accident or something."

"I'm not photogenic," Dorothea confessed. "I usually find a way to hide behind everyone else."

"But I'm a great photographer," Len teased. "Modeling agencies will be clamoring at your door once they see your pictures. Besides, you're young and pretty. You're going to look great."

Young and pretty. His description stayed with her as she popped back into New to You to pick up her purchases. She studied herself in the mirror as the owner retrieved her bags from the back room. Dorothea might not be either of those things, but Dixie could be. The new hair and the make-up she'd begun using made her look different. Granted her cosmetics were only peach blush, eye shadow and lipstick, but she felt better when she used them. Less like the frump Michael thought she was.

Michael.

He stayed on her mind as she walked back to the cottage. She had to let him know she didn't intend to marry him. A note would be perfect but far too rude. She accepted his proposal in person; she needed to reject it the same way.

What would Dixie do?

She began creating a letter to Dixie in her head as she strolled.

Dear Dixie,
I accidentally accepted a marriage proposal to a real jerk because I didn't want to embarrass my father in front of his friends and business partners.

His right-hand assistant is making all the plans for my future, from the wedding itself to where I'll live.

Any suggestion on how to get out of this mess?

Desperate Bride-To-Be

****

The drive to Nashville, one of Rick's least favorite cities for traffic, wasn't as bad as he expected. He stopped at the tourism center and picked up a list of hotels in the city. Marking the five-star ones, he began his hunt for Dorothea.

The hotels were all luxurious. None of them had a guest of Dorothea's name or description staying there alone. None of the managers he spoke to recognized her picture either. Rick figured that a woman of her status, traveling by herself, would be a high priority and therefore memorable. He could only draw one conclusion: she'd been passing through.

Or used a mail service to disguise where she was. But according to those who knew her best, she wasn't the type to come up with a sophisticated scheme.

On an impulse, he went to the city's primary postal mailing center. What he learned there went beyond discouraging. The postal service was consolidating, and mail from other states came to Nashville to be processed and sent to its final destination. Chances were she'd never been in the city at all.

So far, he'd struck out two for two. Rather than waste his time in the city, he did a little sightseeing and had lunch in one of the famous barbecue places. But in the back of his mind, his detective skills were still hard at work.

Women like Dorothea Pfister didn't simply vanish off the face of the earth. Her car was still missing and nothing indicated she'd been taken against her will. Rick's contacts in the Florida state police assured him they'd let him know if she showed up there. Police agencies along the way had received a description of her vehicle and its license plate the day he started the case.

The key to locating her had to be in Cardington. That credit card swipe was the only solid lead he had. He hadn't asked Charley about the transaction. If the thief was still in town, he didn't want to tip his hand.

His room at Lou's was comfortable and well under the per diem he was charging Victor. He had no pressing work for other clients. And if he was on a wild goose chase, at least the weather was a whole lot better in Kentucky than in Chicago.

****

Dorothea studied the printout of her seven dates and the intended destinations. She examined the outfits lying across the bed, a different one for each night. She certainly didn't want to be dressed wrong.

The local basketball coach was picking her up in an hour. Their destination was an informal restaurant down the road by the interstate exit. She chose a short denim skirt, red cowl neck sweater and her cute new boots.

When Date Number One showed up at Lou's front door, Dorothea decided she'd done well. Casual was exactly right. She took a deep breath and prepared for what came next.

"Hello," she said.

"And howdy to you," he responded from on high.

Coach was big. Huge, in fact. Dorothea looked up to meet friendly brown eyes and returned his smile.

"You're a tiny thing." He offered a huge paw for a handshake. "I could tuck you in my pocket." The man wore a grin as wide as the shoulders inside the satiny red jacket with a jaguar embroidered left of the row of snaps. She liked friendly.

"Hope you like meat. We're going to one of the best steakhouses around," he said.

"That sounds lovely."

"Then we better get going."

Coach motioned toward the biggest pick-up truck she'd ever seen. It too was bright red and stood well above the pavement on huge tires. She walked beside him to the passenger door and waited while he swung it open. And gasped when his big hands wrapped around her waist, stiffened as he lifted her onto the wide bucket seat. While his action made sense, Dorothea would have been more comfortable with a little ladder. Or at least some notice of his intentions.

Coach turned the ignition key and the twang of some music foreign to her filled the cab.

"Merle," he said, as if she had a clue who that was. "I love the classics. Johnny, Willie, Don Williams can't go wrong with them."

"Uh, I guess you can't."

"You *are* a country fan, right?"

Dixie offered a small smile. "France is one of my favorites."

Coach let out a huge guffaw.

"You're funny too, not just pretty. We're gonna have a good time tonight."

The songs during the half-hour ride ranged from lost love to inebriation and some dog that helped a prisoner escape. She would have given every penny in her designer purse for a bit of Bach.

"Here we are." Coach pulled too quickly into a parking lot, spewing gravel as he hit the brakes to stop at the end of a long building. The exterior sported faux logs, while neon beer signs shone from the windows. Dorothea took a deep breath and prepared for one more adventure.

The distinct aroma of grilled meat met them as they stepped inside. The noise level made her wince; the hundred or so people there all seemed to be talking at once. Not that she was surprised. The conversations were underscored with the same rowdy music Coach had played in the truck.

At least this restaurant wasn't self-service. Dorothea followed a young woman in a white fringed shirt and black jeans to a table beneath a pair of cattle horns. Coach was mannerly enough to seat her before taking the chair beside hers, stretching his long legs and bumping her calf in the process. Just an accident, she reassured herself, not an attempt at familiarity. He didn't seem to be that sort of man.

The menu was heavy with beef dishes accompanied by some sort of potato and exotic sides like fried macaroni and cheese. She couldn't even imagine what that might taste like.

"Sweet tea," she replied when their server asked what she'd like to drink. Coach ordered a beer; she wasn't surprised when he picked items off the appetizer menu as well.

"Wait till you taste their onion burst," he said, grabbing a handful of peanuts from a small metal bucket in the center of the table. He dropped several of the unshelled nuts in front of her while he began opening the others. The husks created a pile between them.

When in Rome...

Dorothea cracked a shell and slid the nuts out. Following his lead, she popped the peanuts into her mouth and placed the dusty shell on top of Coach's.

"These are tasty," she said, surprised they weren't stale.

"Always are here." Coach dumped a few more in front of her. "They're roasted right here every day."

His steady consumption of the nuts stopped momentarily when a young man stopped by their table.

"Coach!" the youth yelled above the din.

"Hammerhead!" Coach shouted back.

Dorothea watched in appalled fascination as Coach jumped out of his chair and headed toward the young man, banging chests when they met. His next move was to wrangle the newcomer under his arm and rub his knuckles hard across the top of the guy's head. She soon realized she was the only one surprised by what appeared to be some sort of ritual.

She couldn't hear their conversation, but there was a lot of backslapping and laughter.

Whoever Hammerhead was, Coach really liked the loud and uncouth fellow.

The arrival of a golden brown, deep-fried plate of what could only be the lauded onion burst and a basket of chicken wings, also deep-fried, brought Coach back to the table. At his urging,

Dorothea pulled off a few pieces of the onion and put them on the small plate he handed her. She wasn't surprised when he forked two chicken wings and added them to her plate.

"The steaks are grilled to order, so they take a little time," he said. "You're not going to get filled up on that little bit."

That *little bit* was more than her normal meal, but Dorothea wasn't rude enough to tell him. The taste was exceptional for fried food, as Coach had predicted. She ate slowly in the hope he wouldn't notice how little she was ingesting.

"So you're a football coach," she said when the wings were gone.

"Yep, with more wins than any other team in the county."

"That's impressive."

"Not really." Coach grinned. "There's only one other school, and it's pretty small. But we do have a good team. Been to state four times in six years."

"Oh, my, how wonderful." Dorothea had no idea what that meant, but he seemed to be quite proud of the fact.

"My boys are like a machine on that field. Last fall when we went to regionals..."

Coach lost her as he laid out plays, hands flying to punctuate his escalating explanations.

She started when he grabbed the salt and pepper shakers and started moving them around.

"Got your meals, guys." The waitress held a large round tray.

Dorothea stared in dismay at the silver-toned platter the woman set in front of her. She expected a piece or two of roast chicken, not half a bird dominating the plate. The biggest baked potato she'd ever seen lay beside it, a mountain of butter and sour cream melting inside its split halves. Long spears of broccoli covered with melted orange goo finished the presentation. This was not quite what she'd expected when she placed her order.

"Man, that looks good. Almost as good as mine," Coach said.

A huge steak sat in front of him with a layer of peppers and mushrooms covering the surface. Thick fries filled a small plate while a bowl held a heaping portion of the most golden macaroni and cheese she'd ever seen. She watched in fascination as Coach tucked a napkin into his T-shirt neck and sawed into the steak. The man was enthralled with his food.

She tried not to critique hers as she ate. The chicken was slightly dry and could have benefitted from the rosemary orange sauce her father's cook used as a marinade. The overcooked broccoli hung limply from her fork, the thin cheese dripping back onto the platter. But she persevered and managed to down half the meal.

The one good part of the meal was the basket of rolls, crusty on the outside and soft in the middle, with a marvelous honey butter as a spread. The baker certainly deserved kudos.

"So how'd you end up here?"

Coach leaned back in his chair, a second beer cradled in his hands. Despite the napkin bib, a spot of steak sauce glistened on his jacket. Dorothea debated telling him but decided not to chance embarrassing him.

"I stopped for dinner and just stayed."

"Just passing through, huh?" Coach lifted an eyebrow. "Doesn't happen much around here."

"You're native to the area?"

"Born and raised in the county. Got a football scholarship to the state university, managed to squeak through my classes with some help and came back when they offered me a job."

"How fortunate," Dorothea said. "Your need for a position and one opening at the same time was quite a coincidence."

"Nah, they were holding the job for me. My coach was old enough to retire, but he told the school board he wasn't leaving until I was ready to take over. Little reward for my senior year. We didn't lose a single game, and I led the state in yardage."

Dorothea smiled and nodded. Whatever that meant, his pride was obvious.

"Do you have hobbies?" she asked. It was time for a change in subject.

"Fishing, bowling, Battle World," he said. "Set the record for the biggest bass in Lake Edwards a couple of years ago and no one's beat my top score for Battle World yet."

"I'm not certain what that is." In some cases, ignorance was not bliss. "A contact sport?"

"You're not into video games?" Coach seemed astounded. "Battle World is the biggest on-line game there is. I play against people from everywhere, like California and Australia. We've gotta get you hooked up too."

The man played children's games on the computer, the biggest waste of time she could imagine. And bragged about it. She searched for a safer topic.

"Are you reading a good book at the moment?"

"Heck no." Coach gave that now-familiar grin. "I haven't opened a book since I got out of college. If the story's any good, someone will make a movie of it—or even better, a video game. Put some action in it. Like Battle World."

Dorothea kept a smile on her face as he launched into a blow-by-blow description of an on-screen attack that apparently was something to be proud of. She tried to follow as he talked about weapons and secret trapdoors and building battalions, but it proved impossible. Smile and nod, she reminded herself. Just smile and nod.

Relief surged through her when he finally asked if she was ready to go. It was all she could do to stay in her chair until he pulled it back for her. She was so ready for this evening to be over. Then the phone in her purse rang. It was Len.

"I got tied up taking photos of a fender bender on Elm," he apologized. "I'm on my way."

"We were just leaving."

"Let me talk to Coach, okay?"

She handed over the phone and listened to her date's end of conversation, which consisted mostly of "Uh-huh" and "Okay." He handed the phone back.

"What did you two decide?" she asked. "Gonna meet him at the school. He says he'll be there when we get there."

Len had parked at the student entrance. Coach pulled up beside him. Thirty seconds later, they were standing by a goal post. Coach put an arm around her shoulders and tugged her close. One flash shot later, Len had what he needed.

Dorothea watched with longing as the newspaperman left the field and got back into his car.

Naturally, Coach couldn't just take her home. He insisted she tour the locker room and take a better look at the football field. The changing room held the odor of dirty socks and bleach, and the field appeared to be nothing more than grass with lines on it. Still, she tried to react with enthusiasm as Coach recreated moves from his glory years.

"I really must get home," she insisted when he suggested they find a place that sold ice cream. "Deadlines, you know."

He apologized with great haste, making her feel almost bad about trying to escape his presence. Almost. And although she turned her cheek when he went for her mouth, she did allow a good night kiss.

The roar of the pick-up leaving was music to her ears as she stepped into her cottage and locked the door behind her. To think he was one of the top applicants. She made a mental note to thank Len for saving her from the lesser ones.

Her little cottage seemed like paradise when she entered its peaceful interior. Only six more to go, she reminded herself as she set about brewing a cup of nighttime tea. Coach was a very nice man, actually, for someone who liked cowboy music and football. Personally, she couldn't imagine developing a taste for either one.

****

Dorothea slept well but woke up restless. The days before she would absolutely have to go home were dwindling, and she hadn't seen anything of Kentucky at all. She dressed and went over to the house to solicit sightseeing suggestions from Lou. It was no great surprise to find her landlady in the kitchen making cinnamon toast.

"Care to join me?"

"I'd love to." Dorothea couldn't remember the last time she had the treat. Cook had made it for her during her childhood, usually on those days when Dorothea was a little under the weather. The smell of cinnamon brought back memories of Daddy coming to her room to make sure she was feeling better. He would bring her hot cocoa and coffee for himself. They'd visit until he had to get ready to go out to whatever occasion demanded his attention. The staff was very good about making sure she didn't feel alone. One maid in particular kept an eye on her, tucking the blankets around Dorothea and sitting with her until she fell asleep again.

The scent of cinnamon still filled the air when the man from the diner walked in. Lou smiled and asked if he cared to join them.

"Love to." He sat across from Dorothea. "You're spoiling me."

"Everyone needs a hobby," Lou replied as she rose. "Mine happens to involve flour and an oven."

The newcomer smiled at Dorothea.

"I'm Rick Rahall, by the way. I know we met at the diner, but I thought a formal introduction might be nice."

"Dixie White. I didn't realize you were staying here."

"He comes, you go," Lou cut in from by the counter. "I hope you can both be here this evening. I have a hankering for roast beef, but you can't fix just a little. I'd like to invite you to dinner."

"I can't," Dorothea said with real regret. "It's date night number two."

"Oh, that's right." Lou set a plate with two cut slices of toast in front of Rick and joined them. "Who are you going out with tonight?"

"The veterinarian. Dr. Patterson, I believe."
"You'll love Larry. He's one of the most gregarious people you'll ever meet."

****

Rick watched the woman across from him as Lou switched topics to an old gray tomcat she once owned, a patient of Dr. Patterson's. He wouldn't peg Dixie as a thief. On the surface, she appeared to be friendly, honest and trustworthy. She seemed familiar, too, although that was probably because of seeing her picture in the weekly paper. Or maybe a wanted poster at the local post office if she had a criminal past.

Yeah, right. A woman with a criminal past would hang around Cardington for what, the chance to steal some old lady's handbag on the way to church?

Or maybe Dixie was into identity theft. Her cozying up to Lou might be the start of something nefarious. He needed to figure out what her game was, and Dixie inadvertently gave him the perfect way to do it.

"I'd like to explore the area a little," Dixie said to Lou. "Do you have any suggestions?"

"Maybe we can go together," Rick cut in. "I saw something about a bourbon tour."

"Oh, you'd like that," Lou responded with enthusiasm. "Our lady's club went to a distillery last year. It was so interesting even for those of us who don't imbibe."

Lou's endorsement seemed to settle things. His plans for the day had gone from checking out Dixie on the Internet to learning how Kentucky whiskey was made. He loved it when things just fell into place.

****

The limbs of the trees lining the narrow country road were bare, but Dorothea still thought the landscape was beautiful. Rick was an excellent driver. The sun coming through the side window warmed her as they made the short trip from Cardington to the first distillery.

"How many places are on the driving tour?" she asked.

"A half dozen or so," Rick answered. "I thought two might be enough. The process is pretty much the same at all of them."

"Excellent idea."

The well-groomed grounds leading back to numerous large buildings were a surprise.

Rick parked the car, and they walked into the reception and gift shop area to check on tours. Their timing was impeccable. The next one started in just a few minutes. They spent that time taking a quick look at the historical photos and antique equipment on display.

Dorothea was glad she'd opted for walking shoes as their guide led them on a brisk trek from building to building. She had trouble keeping up, not because she was slow but from her fascination with what she viewed.

"It's amazing what it takes to make bottle of bourbon," she commented as they prepared to enter what their guide called the mash room.

If Rick answered, she didn't hear him. The stench of fermenting grain assailed her. She could tell by the faces of her companions they also barely tolerated the smell. She was relieved when they finally passed through and went to the warehouses.

The one they walked into was cool and dark. Barrels were stacked on racks well above her head.

She learned each warehouse had several low-ceilinged floors and how long each barrel had to age before being bottled.

Dorothea didn't care much for hard liquor, but Dixie would certainly join Rick in the samples offered at the end of the tour. She managed her mini-portion but was much happier when the tray of bourbon ball candy came around. She made a mental note to find out where she might buy some as gifts to take home.

"Do you really want to see another one?" Rick asked when they were back in the car.

"Not really. I think they're all the same."

"It's time for lunch anyway. How about we try that place our guide recommended?"

The restaurant, located in one of the town's most historic buildings, made Dorothea feel like she'd stepped back in time. The brick interior walls and scarred wooden floors were obviously original. The tables and chairs were representations of colonial times, each covered with a checked tablecloth.

Everything on the menu sounded wonderful. Dorothea studied the regional specialties.

"Smothered chicken," she read aloud. "Golden fried with a unique combination of spices and covered with rich white gravy. That sounds like an invitation to a heart attack."

"Sounds great to me." Rick closed his menu. "That's what I'm having."

"You don't have a dinner date in a few hours. I think I'd better stick to something lighter. The club sandwich sounds good."

Their conversation was casual as they waited for their food to arrive. They talked mostly about the distillery and the decor of the restaurant. It wasn't until they compared notes on the pie that Dorothea realized how comfortable she was with Rick. She hadn't felt self-conscious even once during their several hours together.

"Ready for dessert?" their server asked as she came for their empty plates. "We have lemon pie made the same way the Shaker believers did at their religious settlement a hundred years ago. It's a little tart but tasty."

Dorothea knew Dixie would be game for something new, so she ordered a piece. So did Rick.

Dorothea laughed when he tasted the pie and his face tightened in surprise.

"She's right. It's got a definite bite to it." Rick waved toward her untouched piece. "Go ahead. Try it."

Dorothea cut off a tiny bit from the point of the slice and slipped it into her mouth. Wow. Tangy was too mild a description.

"It's good anyway," she said.

"Because you're sweet enough to offset the lemons," he teased, leaning forward and smiling at her. "I've had a great time today."

"Me too. Despite the stinky part."

Rick laughed and threaded his fingers through hers.

"But without the mash there would be no bourbon. No bourbon, no candy. Life's full of surprises."

"Yeah." Like sitting in a historic inn with an intriguing stranger instead of following chapter and verse of Patrice's punish the bride book.

The sun's westward descent was underway as they started back toward Cardington.

"How did you end up here?" Rick asked as they drove down the country road.

Dorothea was far more confident now than she had been in Len's office, creating Dixie.

She offered her alter ego's story, hoping it wasn't thin enough to bring probing questions.

"I'm a bit of a wanderer," she said. "I grew up in the house my parents inherited from my grandparents. While they were perfectly content to stay put, I knew there had to be more to the world. So once I was on my own, I set out to see it."

"Floating here and there, just a free spirit," he suggested.

Ooh, that sounded like Dixie. Dorothea decided to go with it.

"Life is meant to be experienced. When I find the right place, I'll put down roots. Until then, I intend to enjoy each day as it comes."

Dorothea developed her story as Rick continued to ask more questions. She gave the same answer to him as she had Len about her last place of residence. She made up jobs she'd held and even regaled him with her tenure as a hostess in a restaurant that didn't exist.

"That's enough about me," she finally said. "What brought you here?"

"Business." His answer was succinct. "I'm a researcher. My work keeps me on the road, but I like settling down someplace quiet when I work."

"You're doing research in Cardington?" Dorothea couldn't imagine what there was to find there.

"Center of operations. It's an easy drive to the places I need to visit."

"Oh."

She still couldn't imagine why he fixed on the tiny town as his headquarters, but she supposed it made sense to him. After all, hadn't she ended up here by accident as well?

Lou greeted them with the announcement that she'd made carrot cake with cream cheese frosting while they were gone. Dorothea turned down the offer, not because it didn't sound delicious but because her date would be arriving in two hours.

She still had to take a shower, fiddle with make-up, and prepare for the evening ahead.

Tonight's new acquaintance was the area's only veterinarian. According to Len's schedule, the plan was to attend a weekly potluck and dance at the American Legion hall. At least she could dance. The years of lessons her father had insisted on included the ballroom variety.

She was waiting in the warm foyer of Lou's house five minutes before he was to arrive. Four minutes before he should be ringing the doorbell, Lou's house phone rang. She came back from answering it with a message.

"That was Doc," she said. "He's just now leaving the clinic. Said it shouldn't be long."

Fifteen minutes later, Dorothea accepted the renewed offer of cake. She was hungry; it had been a long time since lunch. Half an hour later, after she decided he had stood her up, the man finally arrived.

Dr. Patterson wasn't what she had expected. He was a little older, balder and a bit distant. Or maybe he was worried about his clients and thought she had something communicable. Like hoof-and-mouth disease.

"Got a stop to make on the way," he said after introducing himself as Just Call Me Larry. "Hope you don't mind."

"That's perfectly fine."

"Really, I'll just be a minute."

Since they were going to a dance, she hadn't expected to be driving out into the country in a van with Dr. P's Mobile Animal Hospital on the side. Thin sunlight still illuminated the rural area spotted with fields of something. Corn, maybe?

"Here we are."

Dorothea expected to remain inside the van, but Just Call Me Larry insisted she go with him. Her heart sank when they started walking toward a barn. Didn't the man know what could happen to good suede shoes? But she'd agreed to this, she reminded herself. And surely she wouldn't have to go inside.

Larry waved her ahead of him when they reached the yawning space normally covered by a wide metal door. Taking a deep breath, she stepped in. To her surprise, the odor was negligible, and the place was clean and neat. Her shoes were safe.

"Thanks for coming by, Doc." A woman in sweat pants and tennis shoes with white hair carelessly bundled on top of her head leaned against a wooden gate. She glanced inside before saying, "Clara's just not acting right."

"She's like any expectant mother. Ready to get this over with."

Dorothea watched as he climbed over the gate and into the stall. The woman waved her closer. Dorothea looked in to see Larry cuddling a white goat. He frowned as he ran his hands across the creature's swollen middle.

"Who's my good girl?" he muttered. "You are, aren't you?"

Clara butted against his hip and brought a chuckle from her visitor. "Nothing in my pocket this time," he said. "You're out of luck."

Once his examination was over, he climbed back to where Dorothea stood next to the goat's owner. She listened as he explained Clara could give birth at any time and he expected a call at the first sign of trouble.

"She'll have a bunch," he said. "I wouldn't be surprised if she gave you four kids. Maybe even five."

They climbed back into the truck with gifts. Larry had a tin of goat's milk candy made that day while Dorothea had a round ball of scented *soap with goat's milk as the prime ingredient.*

"Nettie sells her stuff at the farmers' market all summer or through my clinic and the feed store in cold weather. It gives her a little extra money, but more important, it keeps her busy." He circled past the barn door where the woman stood, stopping to call out with a grin, "Sure you don't need a cat? Got a couple nice ones that got dropped off."

"I have plenty," she called back. "I'm running out of mice for them to catch."

They rode in silence halfway back to town, the hum of the tires the only music around them.

"She seems nice," Dorothea offered, trying to start a conversation.

"Oh, Clara's one of the best. This is her second litter, and I hope it goes easier than the last one. If I hadn't been there, she would have died."

Dorothea had been referring to Nettie, but she didn't have a chance to clarify things. Larry launched into an explanation of goat keeping that would have been great if she was writing a dissertation. He had switched from goats to why house pets shouldn't eat people food by the time they reached the white-sided building with about two-dozen cars in the parking lot.

"Hope you don't mind if I make a call," Larry said with a note of apology in his voice. "I forgot to remind Nettie not to let Clara eat anything this close to delivery."

A few minutes later, they walked into the hall where long tables held a number of covered dishes and pans. The scents arising from them were divine.

"Ah, it's Miss White." A middle-aged woman in jeans and a red pullover sweater stopped them as they walked toward a knot of people. "Or do you prefer your first name?"

"Either is fine."

"Then I'll call you Dixie and you call me Melinda. I'm the pastor down at Grace Church, which always organizes the meal."

Dorothea didn't know why she was surprised the woman was a minister. Probably because the main-line church she'd attended all her life only had male clergymen, usually older with a willingness to play golf with the most influential members.

Melinda clapped her hands to get the attention of the group of thirty or so.

"This is Dixie," she announced, "who has joined us for her date with Larry. Now let's pray."

Dorothea took a bit of everything, whether she recognized the contents of the dish or not, just to be polite. Larry scooped up big spoonsful of his favorites and led her over to a round table with two seats together. She wasn't surprised when the conversation centered on Larry and his veterinary practice. Or that a large part of that conversation was from fellow diners soliciting advice. He took it all in stride, which went in the plus column. He still had to do a little more to erase the negative of starting their date in a goat barn.

The band had begun to play by the time Len walked in with his camera. Dorothea discovered her dance lessons had a serious omission when Larry took her hand and led her onto the floor. Instead of taking her in his arms, he stood next to her at the end of a long line of people. The music started and she was lost.

"Just do what I do," he called above the sound. "Line dancing's easy once you get the hang of it."

She was relieved to sit the next one out after her date excused himself and headed for the restroom. Len stopped over to make sure she was comfortable and show her the photos he'd taken. The man had talent. She actually looked like she knew what she was doing on the dance floor.

The band began a waltz, which was in her comfort zone. She sat at the table, tapping her toes, since Larry was still gone. She started at a hand laid on her shoulder and a now-familiar voice asking, "Would you care to dance?"

She looked into Rick's smiling face.

Dixie would, she reminded herself. She was a free spirit. She wouldn't sit around just waiting for Larry's return.

"I'd love to."

Dorothea stepped into Rick's arms. The cotton of his shirt whispered against her arm as she put one hand at the back of his neck. Her head came just to his shoulder, as if they were meant to dance together. His left hand was light at the curve of her back; his right held hers with just the right pressure.

The tension she'd felt at his request left as they moved across the floor. Rick danced well, with a natural grace. She laid her head against his chest and felt the vibration as he hummed along with the music.

Closing her eyes, she let herself relax against him. Comfortable. That's how he made her feel, as if they were alone on the dance floor. As though this song of love lost and regained was just for them. Her senses heightened as they moved to the music. His body was warm against hers where they touched, his breath light and gentle across her hair. The aftershave he wore was slightly spicy—altogether masculine.

A sense of loss swept over her as Rick stepped back and cool air came between them. How could the music end? How could she dance with Larry now that she'd had this moment with *this* man?

"Thank you." Rick's smile, as if they shared a secret, sent tremors through her.

If only he was one of her seven. These few moments would have been the best date of all.

"You looked good out there." Larry greeted Dorothea with a wide smile when she returned to the table. "Sorry I was gone so long. I wanted to check on Clara while I had a chance."

"Clara's a patient," Dorothea explained to Rick before introducing the two men.

"One of my favorites," Larry added. "Great goat. Good conformation, produces more than a gallon of milk a day. And she has such a sweet personality."

Dorothea hid a smile as Rick stood nodding as her date kept on talking. The men she knew wouldn't be so polite. Finally, Rick managed to interrupt.

"Nice meeting you," he said to Larry before turning to Dorothea to say, "Thanks for the dance. I enjoyed it."

She kept her eyes on Rick as he made his way through the crowd to the door, surprised he was leaving so soon. His departure wasn't because of a lack of partners. There were more women than men here tonight, and a number of them watched as he headed to the door.

She and Larry joined the others on the dance floor for the band's last song. Once it was over, Larry led her to the one of the tables where Melinda handed him several takeout boxes and foil-wrapped items.

"He's one of those bachelors who'd live on cheese sandwiches if you let him," the pastor confided. "I always send leftovers with him."

The delay made them among the last to leave. But that didn't stop Larry in what she now realized was probably a perennial quest.

"Now you sure wouldn't like a nice cat?" he called to several couples as they paused at the exit door.

"No!" came a unanimous answer. Dorothea had a feeling he was stuck with those cats for life, either his or theirs.

Back at Lou's, he walked her from the van to her door. They ended their time together with a firm handshake and Larry's call as he walked away. "Hey, remember, I've got cats!"

Dorothea laughed and waved goodbye. Two dates down, five to go. Once this week and the contest were over, she simply had to resign and go back to Chicago. Absolutely must.

****

"She's probably dead." Michael stared into his tumbler of golden liquor and shook his head. "It's been two weeks, Victor. Two weeks."

"Dorothea is not dead," Patrice retorted in a sharp tone. "She's being silly and muddleheaded. She's just looking for some great adventure before the two of you marry. She's been so sheltered all her life that she has no common sense."

"Stop, you two!" Victor shot a quelling glance at one and then the other. "Her note is reassuring, and Rahall is checking every avenue."

"Taking your money for nothing is more like it."

The whiskey fed Michael's courage.

"I'm telling you, something has happened to her. Something terrible."

"Say that again and I'll deck you," Victor growled. "I'm beginning to believe you're the reason she's staying away. That child never gave me a bit of trouble until you started pushing for a fast wedding."

"She's lucky I'm willing to take her. She doesn't hold the prize for beauty and brains, you know."

Victor jumped up from his chair and charged to the settee where Michael had settled in.

His hands curled into fists as he towered over the man, his face red.

"Don't malign my daughter again. She's worth a dozen of you, Butterwell. I think it's time for you to leave. Patrice, call the man a cab."

"I can drive just fine." Michael pulled himself up, the liquor sloshing from his glass.

"Your drunken ass is being taken home. I'd suggest you think about giving up the booze if you still want your partnership. And my daughter. You're very close to losing both right now." Victor slumped down on the settee Michael had vacated and buried his face in his hands.

Where was Dorothea? Was his little girl safe?

Those questions were still on his mind as he tried to sleep each night and when he woke every morning. He had to believe she was all right. That note was definitely her handwriting. The wording was hers as well. He patted the pocket that held his cell phone. He'd give anything to hear her voice right now, anything at all. This big house and his success meant nothing. He'd done it all for Dorothea, to make sure she'd have everything she needed or wanted.

"Are you all right?" Patrice sat next to him and laid her hand on his thigh. "That was a very ugly moment."

"I shouldn't have let my temper get the best of me. Michael's a good lawyer, and I know he's only saying those things because he's sick with worry about Dorothea. I just want her home."

"I know." Patrice leaned her head on Victor's shoulder. "Your detective will find her. Life will be back to normal. Now relax. It won't help a thing if you have a heart attack." Victor patted Patrice's hand and smiled.

"I couldn't get through this without you," he said. "Thank you for being here. It means so much to me."

"I know," Patrice murmured. "You know I love Dorothea, too. You two are my family. I could never take her mother's place, but I'd like to think I've helped her become the woman she is."

"Ah, Patrice, you know you have." He tipped her face toward him. "What would I ever do without you?"

Chapter Seven

Dixie White was an enigma. The woman Rick held in his arms last night had no history. He searched the Internet trying to confirm anything she'd told him and came up empty. Even the restaurant she so vividly described was a figment of her imagination.

He propped the picture of Dorothea Pfister up against the newspaper photo of Dixie. Yeah, there were some similarities. The shape of the face, the color of the eyes. But Dorothea didn't have that spark evident even in a photo of Dixie. The missing heiress was serene, almost somber. Dixie had a charming smile; the tip of her head invited you to join her on some adventure.

Yet somewhere they'd crossed paths. He was certain Dixie had used the Pfister woman's credit card but only that once. Only for a small purchase that wouldn't even register as money spent for the missing woman. So what was she up to?

These dates worried him a little. Could be she'd conned the newspaper into being an inadvertent part of her scam. If she ripped those guys off and headed out of town, the editor would have his feet held to the fire. Rick felt an obligation to warn the man. Yet if he were wrong, he would destroy Dixie's reputation for no reason.

He sighed, gathered the paper and photo and dropped them in the drawer. This was supposed to be easy cash, one quick assignment. Doubt and dead ends dogged him. Even though he had nothing to report, he needed to call Victor.

A knock on his door delayed him. He opened it to find Dixie there in jeans and a bright tie-dyed T-shirt.

"Lou's running out of sugar and flour so we're going to the supermarket," she said. "She wanted to see if you'd like us to pick anything up for you."

Here was the perfect opportunity to get to know Dixie better.

"Actually, I'd like to ride along if you don't mind. Get out of the house for a while."

"I'm sure Lou wouldn't mind." Dixie looked pleased. Chalk one up to the famed Rahall charm. "We're leaving in a few minutes."

The gentlemanly thing was to allow Dixie the front seat, which gave him the chance to stretch out on the back seat of the older SUV. That also allowed the distinct advantage of being able to listen in on the women's conversation, which included a dissection of Dixie's two dates so far. He expected a few snarky comments when she began the recaps, but the most negative thing he heard was there was no chemistry with either of them.

He felt a glow of satisfaction. He felt a definite spark when they danced and was pretty sure Dixie had too. Rick would have pursued it if the situation had been different. If his investigation might not land her in court and him testifying against her.

"Do you have a lady friend at home?" Lou looked at him through the rear view mirror.

"Not at the moment."

"So you're both single."

Rick didn't care much for the contented tone in Lou's observation. The last thing he needed was for the older woman to decide to play matchmaker.

"I, for one, am very happy that way," Dixie interjected. Rick hoped that would cut off any attempts by Lou to make them into a couple. The older woman did drop the subject, much to his relief. He far preferred her stories of the old days of Cardington to personal questions.

Rick returned home with a six-pack of Ale 8, a regional soft drink Lou insisted he had to try, a nice assortment of snack foods, and no new information on Dixie except she loved strawberries and hated grapefruit. He also got the feeling she'd like to have a night off from her dating schedule. He didn't blame her. He'd only been on one blind date in his life and that was a disaster. He couldn't imagine seven in a row.

Rick made a point to be sitting by the fire when Dixie came in from the cottage a few minutes before her date was due to arrive. He wanted to see this guy and how she interacted with him. Important to confirm or rule out his suspicions, he told himself, ignoring the niggling bit of jealousy he felt when she floated in wearing a full-skirted dress with a little sweater over it. She carried a coat over her arm.

"You look pretty," he said.

"Thank you." She gave him a shy smile as if she didn't hear compliments often. But her smile faded when the doorbell chimed.

"Wish me luck," she muttered when Lou walked over to open it. Figuring that was a rhetorical request, Rick stayed silent.

The man who entered with obvious reluctance wore a fleece-lined work jacket, jeans and scuffed western boots. His attire was a definite contrast to Dixie's fancy outfit; Rick wondered where this guy was taking her. To a cow-milking contest, maybe?

"Have a good time!" Lou called as the pair went out the door. Rick turned down her offer of brownies and milk, pleading a need to catch up on some work. He planned to kick back and catch up with his favorite TV show on his computer, and turn in early. Or start in on the new thriller novel he'd bought in Nashville and stay up to see what time Dixie got home from her evening out with the plowboy.

****

Stella had warned her Freddie Moatz was a little bashful. That was like saying a July Fourth fireworks display was a trifle noisy.

"Uh, you like pizza, right?"

"Sure." Dorothea kept her single-syllable response soft, as if she was coaxing a kitten from under the couch.

"My daddy always says eatin' together is a good way to get to know somebody."

"Your father sounds like a wise man."

"He knows all about cows too."

"That's nice."

Freddie wasn't unattractive despite the ruddiness of his cheeks and the cowlick on the crown of his head. She might not have noticed the unruly strands of hair if he didn't have a habit of smoothing them every couple of minutes. His eyes were a bright blue, not unexpected in someone with his bright yellow hair. She figured he was about her own age, thirty or so.

"We're here." Freddie steered the older yet well-maintained sedan into a parking place near the door. Dorothea stepped out of the car when he got out and stood by its grille. She couldn't expect every date to have impeccable manners, she reminded herself.

This was a seat-yourself place. Freddie chose a booth by a window in the back of the room. She wasn't sure whether he wanted them to have a little privacy or if Freddie didn't like being around other people. She encouraged him to order for them both, nodding her head in agreement when he asked if she'd like a cola.

"My daddy always says drinking is for at home," he said as the waitress carried a pitcher of beer past them. "Do you like beer?"

"Not particularly." Dorothea wrinkled her nose.

"I think it stinks," Freddie confided.

That's where the conversation ended until their pizza and breadsticks arrived. Dorothea spent the idle time watching Freddie play with the paper from his straw and by watching the other diners. Some of them looked familiar. Wow. She'd been here long enough to recognize a few of the good people of Cardington. She ought to send her father another note in the morning. She certainly didn't want him arriving in Florida and wondering why she wasn't there yet. She had to be vague. He would never believe she was living on her own let alone that she had a job.

"This is very good." She took another bite. The pepperoni and sausage topping was quite different from the vegetarian, four-cheese style the club served but tasty nonetheless. Freddie seemed to enjoy it immensely, putting away slice after slice and nearly all the breadsticks. Len arrived as promised to take a photo. Freddie scooted to the end of the booth, against the wall; Dorothea did the same on her side. The result was a picture of the two of them separated by a table and an empty pizza pan.

Len left, and their drinks were refilled.

"I understand that you're in agriculture," she said.

"Dairy farm. My father started it."

"And you run it now?"

"Since three years ago. His back got bad."

"Do you have a lot of cows?" Carrying on a sustained conversation with this guy was like pulling teeth, slow and painful.

"Fifty head."

"That's a lot to take care of."

"My father always says hard work never hurt anybody. Morning milking's at six.
Evening at six too."

"That sounds interesting," she said, only a little lie.

"It's okay."

Dorothea could only carry on an inquisition for so long. They once again lapsed into silence. She was relieved when they were able to leave. Freddie was a cautious driver, which translated into slow.

Eventually they reached Lou's, Freddie said goodbye and Dorothea climbed out of the car and walked to the porch alone.

She was surprised to see both Lou and Rick sitting by the fireplace until she realized how short the date had been. Although she was too full for carrot cake, she accepted the offer to join them. Voluntary conversation was exactly what she needed after ninety minutes of Mr. Bashful.

"How's your research going?" she asked Rick.

"Slow." He shrugged. "Happens sometimes. How's your column writing?"

"Going well."

"The only thing more scintillating around here would be you two talking about the weather." Lou got up to poke the fire. "Don't you listen to music or watch movies?"

Dorothea joined Rick in laughter, although she wondered how she could have reached twenty-nine without knowing what normal people talked about. Her conversations with Michael were always about him—his glory years of high school basketball, his hot cases, his plans for the future. She might have been the living room sofa for all he cared. Even when he did ask her how her day had been, he never waited to hear her answer.

As the fire died down, the three of them discussed favorite books. Dorothea was surprised to learn Rick and she had similar tastes in literature. She didn't even notice when Lou dropped out of the discussion of suspense novels versus mysteries. So it was a surprise when the grandfather's clock in the adjacent room struck eleven.

"My bedtime," Lou announced. "You two are welcome to stay up all night if you'd like, but I'm getting up early to make cinnamon rolls for breakfast. I'm a morning person, you know."

Dorothea said her own goodnights. Stepping out the back door, she walked with a light step down the short path to the cottage. The evening might have started out slow, but she enjoyed the rest of it immensely. Maybe too much. She was going to miss Rick when she was gone.

****

"So far so good." Len poured several teaspoons of sugar into his mug and stirred. He'd already been drinking coffee when Dorothea walked into the diner to join him for lunch. She'd slept well the night before, but he sported bags beneath his eyes.

"Tonight means we're halfway done," she replied.

"We have one change," Len said. "Tomorrow's dinner date has become breakfast instead. Bachelor Number Five had a change in schedule. Is that okay with you?"

"Sure. I'm flexible."

As Dixie anyway. In her real life, Dorothea lived by a planner, most of the entries demanded by Patrice or Michael. There was no room for spontaneity.

"I thought you might like an evening off. You've been a trooper with this every night thing."

"I'm enjoying it. You'd be surprised how much I'm learning about Cardington. I'm starting to get to know people too."

"The beauty of a small town. Ah, here's our food."

Len practically inhaled his cheeseburger and fries. The aroma was delicious. Dorothea pretended she didn't care as she ate the small chef's salad she hoped would serve as an antidote to all the big meals she'd already had this week. Since he finished first, he regaled her with stories from the newspaper—including a number of hilarious ones featuring Stella. Dorothea was beginning to realize how hard it would be, when the time came, to leave. She was falling in love with this small town.

But no chance with any of the men she'd met, she assured Len.

"They've all been quite nice, but there's been absolutely no spark," she said. "That's a good thing, don't you think? This is supposed to be a fun experience, not a competition."

"Be ready if tonight's shows up with a bouquet. It won't be a romantic gesture. More like part of a marketing campaign."

"Oh, yeah, this is the florist."

"He's in Rotary club with me. Nice guy. Knows all about flowers."

Bill Studevant did indeed know all about them, she discovered after he picked her up that evening. She half expected a delivery van to take her away, but Bill drove a low-slung red sports car. He began apologizing as soon as he started the engine.

"Finished a wedding today," he said, his tone nasal. "The bride wanted exotic flowers. They cost the earth but she was willing to pay. I think *ah-choo!* that I may be allergic to some of them."

He barely got the last word out before he sneezed again, this time six in a row. Luckily, he was driving slowly, and there was no other traffic on the street; it didn't matter that he drifted a little until he finished. Dorothea was prepared to grab the wheel if he had another sneezing fit.

"My apologies. I popped some antihistamines before I left the house, but I guess they haven't kicked in yet." His voice was thick. "I'm sure it won't be long now."

Dorothea's heart sank when he made a familiar turn. She did not want to go to that steakhouse again. Ever. Bill kept driving and, a mile or so further, pulled into the parking lot of a low building set back and partially concealed by greenery. A small sign simply read Parker's.

She felt comfortable the moment they walked in. A string trio was playing on a small stage at the back of a large dining area broken up by banquettes. The host greeted Bill by name and they were immediately escorted to one of the semi-private dining areas. Chilled wine already rested in an ice bucket and a long-stemmed red rose lay above one place setting.

Dorothea was impressed.

Following Bill's recommendation, she ordered the crusted chicken with garlic mashed potatoes, corn soufflé and asparagus spears. Every bite was as delicious as he had promised.

They ate in leisure, allowing time to talk.

Bill talked mostly. Dorothea learned that he worked six days a week and closed the shop for two weeks each summer so he could rent a cabin in Canada for a little escape from the craziness of running his own business. She also learned he sold more flowers for Mother's Day than on Valentine's Day, which surprised her.

"If this was early May, I'd be too swamped for a lovely evening like this," he said. "No one knows what to buy their mothers so they send flowers. Prom time can be crazy too. All those poor boys buying corsages for girls who are so demanding. Last year I created enough hot pink and lime green nosegays to last me a lifetime. But enough about me. What's your favorite flower, dear?"

"Roses, I guess." She did appreciate the one she just received.

"Ah, roses. A perennial favorite. My grandmother was quite partial to tea roses. She had the most beautiful bush in the side yard. The blooms were as pink as pink could be and the scent was incredible."

That led into another story by Bill of a couple who bought each other roses on every anniversary, one for each year.

"They're absolute darlings, been married nearly forty years. What's amusing is that she always charges the flowers she orders and he pays the bill for all of them. But it's the sentiment that counts, I suppose, and not who holds the checkbook."

Dessert, the most fantastic cheesecake Dorothea ever tasted, made up for Bill's detailed explanation of the new trends in flower arranging. Listening to men talk about themselves was the story of her life thanks to both Daddy and Michael. A fantastic meal like this wasn't. She expected this quality in Chicago, but not out here. Bill did know how to treat a lady.

She allowed a hug after he walked her to the door, but it was like embracing her brother.

Or how she imagined it felt if she had a brother.

She glanced at the house as she headed for the cottage. The only lights were upstairs, in separate windows. Apparently both Rick and Lou had gone to their rooms.

Dorothea wasn't tired. She took a long soaking bath, her mind not on the recent date but the lively discussion on books with Rick. He was intelligent, he was funny, and he made her feel at ease. If only Michael had one of those traits. Okay, she'd give him being smart. He just didn't use his brain as well as Rick did.

She turned on the gas logs in the fireplace and settled on the divan with a cup of tea and a magazine she bought at the grocery store. No one who knew her would believe she was about to study tips on make-up and how to flirt. She smiled to herself. Here in Kentucky she was Dixie, and Dixie was all about that stuff.

A whole lot of information was crammed between the covers, an education on glossy, perfumed-scented pages. By the time she tossed the magazine onto the sofa and went to bed, she knew how to look ten pounds thinner by dressing differently, the hottest new TV shows for the upcoming season and how to take care of her skin at any age. What she hadn't learned was how to gracefully get out of her engagement and discover whether what she thought was a connection with Rick could become something real great.

Sleep came easily. The warmth of the radiator beside the bed kept her cozy, and the slice of illumination from the streetlight made her feel safe. She realized, as she dozed off, that she felt less alone living here by herself than she did back home with Daddy. That was a sad commentary on her life.

Previous life. Things would be different once she got back to Chicago.

Chapter Eight

Eight in the morning was way too early for any kind of date. Dorothea set her alarm for seven just in case she hit the snooze button and overslept a little. The very idea of putting on makeup before her first cup of coffee was appalling, yet she managed it. She dressed casually, since she was meeting this new man at the diner. Her butt looked pretty good in her secondhand jeans, she decided after checking herself out in the mirror.

The air was nippy, but Dorothea walked to the diner anyway. She was determined to keep her resolution to get more exercise. The chill made her steps a little brisker, and she found she had arrived first.

She picked a table near the front and by the wide window. She watched traffic until an extended bed pick-up pulled in and parked. The guy who swung out of it was tall and lean with a camouflage jacket, jeans and orangish-brown work boots. Mike Henderson, if his photo was accurate.

He spotted her as soon as he walked in and began to apologize before he sat down.

"We've got a guy out with kidney stones," he said with a wide yawn. "I'm picking up his shifts this week. Sixteen-hour shifts aren't a favorite but the money's too good to turn down."

"So you've been working since yesterday afternoon?"

"Got to. There's only four journeymen machinists at the plant and the others have families. Me, all I have to go home to is my dog."

He yawned again, calloused hand across his mouth. When the server came to take their order, he asked her if she could leave a carafe of coffee instead of refilling a cup. The woman's quick agreement made Dorothea think this was a fairly common occurrence.

His comment about owning a dog clicked. Here was someone who might have advice for the advice columnist. She outlined the reader's question about the neighboring cat and the flower bed. Mike took a big swig of coffee, stretched his shoulders as if he was stiff from finally sitting and said, "Is that letter from Maribelle Betts?"

"No idea. The writer didn't use a name."

"Probably Maribelle. First of all, she doesn't like cats to begin with. And she treats that dog of hers like a fairy princess." He leaned forward. "Tell her this. Get some mothballs and put them around her azaleas. Pull the curtain so her precious pooch can't see the cats. That's all it will take."

"Thanks."

She waved off a refill as Mike topped off his cup again. The poor man looked exhausted.

She wondered how many times he took those extra hours so his fellow workers could go home.

"It's nice of you to work so hard," she said.

"Nah, it's not a matter of nice. I intend to retire as soon as I get twenty years in and buy a place down in Florida. While all those guys are working their butts off at the plant, I'll be on a boat fishing. Work now, play later. That's my plan."

Dorothea wasn't sure how to respond. In her world, men rarely took retirement. They might not go into the office as often, but no one voluntarily gave up the reins. Of course, Mike wasn't in charge. She supposed that made a difference.

"Do you like what you do?" she asked, truly curious.

Mike shrugged. "Beats flipping burgers. Money's good and the work is steady."

Wealth was something she'd always taken for granted. Daddy gave her everything she needed from cash when she wanted it to paying for the credit cards she used. Even now she was relying on what she'd taken from the desk.

"How about you?" Mike asked. "This a good job?"

She did have a job, she suddenly realized. She'd still been considering it a social experiment, but it was more than that. She had responsibilities. If she fulfilled them, she received a check each month. A sudden elation filled her. She was a wage earner without her father's influence.

A sudden awareness of the world around her colored the conversation. She was eager to know more about life with goals.

Len showed up with his camera right before they left. She moved over to sit next to Mike, both of them holding up coffee cups when Len pressed the shutter. This portrait would be two working folks sharing an ordinary breakfast.

Her internal discovery buoyed her throughout the day. She stopped by the newspaper office to learn that a huge stack of letters awaited her. The series of dates was the talk of the town, and it seemed like nearly everyone either had a situation for Dixie to solve or simply wanted to make a comment. Walking home with the fat manila envelope, Dorothea felt popular for the first time in her life.

She stopped stock still in the middle of the sidewalk, a sudden realization washing over her.

She didn't want to go home. She wanted to stay part of this sweet little town, one small thread in the fabric of its life. How in the world could she tell Daddy?

****

Rick made his daily calls. His Florida contact assured him no one had spotted either Dorothea or the Saab. The credit card hadn't been used again, which surprised him. Usually thieves tended to max out stolen credit cards and then trash them. Victor said the one Dorothea carried had no limit, yet one charge of a hundred bucks was all that had been put on it.

Despite his reluctance, Rick made the call to the man who was paying his per diem.

Victor was far more patient than Rick expected. But one of these days, he was going to blow up. A man can only hold back his emotions for so long.

The sadness in Victor's voice was depressing. Rick never had a great longing for kids but he could understand how painful not knowing could be. He'd done his share of talking with parents and spouses in similar situations.

"I'm trusting that no news is good news," Victor said. "Three weeks is a long time, but my little girl has a good head on her shoulders. I'm sure she's too smart to fall for some guy's line." He hesitated before adding, "I don't want to worry Patrice or Michael, but I wonder if she's had an emotional breakdown. That sudden proposal and so much pressure may have been too much for her."

Rick hadn't considered that possibility, but once Victor voiced his fear, he knew he had to follow up. A new avenue at least gave him an excuse for continuing to take the man's money.

"Be discreet," Victor requested when Rick said he'd start making inquiries. "She's a sensitive child. If she's had a nervous breakdown it would humiliate her for others to know."

"I'll be careful," Rick assured him. At the verge of saying goodbye, a sudden request occurred to him. He asked for the name of Dorothea's two closest friends.

"Michael is her closest confidante, of course, and she's always been fond of Patrice."

Victor hesitated. Rick heard a background noise as if the other man was rifling through files.

"She stays in touch with a friend from college, and she has lunch occasionally with the daughter of one of my partners. I'll have Patrice text you that information."

A strange sadness settled over Rick as he hung up, an empathy for Dorothea he hadn't expected. If her boyfriend and her dad's whatever were those most near and dear to her, the woman's life was emptier than he could imagine. No wonder she stayed hidden. Spending time with those two and realizing what they thought of Dorothea half made him want to give up the search. He could call a couple of hospitals where he was sure she hadn't checked in, send the disappointing result to Victor and resign from the case.

Could. But he wasn't a quitter. She was somewhere. And he couldn't help but suspect Dixie White had some sort of knowledge. He thought about sneaking into the cottage she occupied, but Lou was far too alert for him to pull that off. The woman was like a mama bear when it came to Dixie. She knew chapter and verse about every one of the men Dixie was going out with as well as their mothers and sisters. She was a walking encyclopedia when it came to the people of Cardington and Wolfton County.

Her scrutiny was a boon for Dixie's safety but hard to overcome for an investigator. He'd hoped Dixie would invite him over for drinks or something. So far, though, nothing.

He didn't know what kind of car she drove or even if she had one. A small garage behind the cottage provided parking for its occupant. His car went into a carport attached to the Victorian style two-car garage Lou used.

He never saw Dixie drive though. She walked wherever she went. The day they went to the supermarket, they took Lou's old boat.

His phone beeped. The expected text had arrived. He saved it to archives and found Lou to tell her he'd be out most of the day. He had two goals: To check the better hotels and hospitals in Louisville, just in case Dorothea only got that far, and to tour the Louisville Slugger bat factory. If he was going on a wild goose chase, he ought to have some fun while he was doing it.

****

Lou was alone in the house, watching some talk show with screaming women and fathers denying paternity when Dorothea went to find her. After a little nap, Dorothea had tackled the letters. One or two were obviously foolish, some were serious, but a lot of them were simple notes to say hello and how are you to the newspaper's addition. She hadn't realized such old fashioned courtesies still existed. Or maybe they only did in places like this.

"Hello, dear." Lou looked up and muted the TV.

"I wanted to let you know I was going out for a bit. I thought I'd do a little shopping. Would you like to come along?"

"Thank you but no. You might want to head to the outlet mall. They have all the shops for young girls like you."

"Outlet mall?" Dorothea echoed.

"Stores with discounts on all the top brands," Lou explained. "I like to go window shopping and then have lunch in the nice little café in the center. It has excellent tuna fish sandwiches."

Since she was all about new experiences, Dorothea jotted down Lou's directions. The drive down the interstate seemed to take no time at all and she had no problem finding the place.

It loomed over the countryside, a virtual paradise for the credit generation.

She walked from shop to shop, snapping up bargains right and left. The café was her destination when she began to tire. Lou was right; the tuna salad was rich and creamy with just the right amount of crunchy chopped celery and onion. The red velvet cake tempted Dorothea, but she decided against a slice. She did have another date tonight, after all.

Who was it again? Oh, the life insurance salesman. Something Hammond. No, Hamilton like the president. Ted, she believed. Ted Hamilton.

****

Dorothea was waiting in Lou's foyer, dressed in her new black slacks, red cowl-neck sweater and a heart-dotted white scarf in honor of the upcoming Valentine's Day holiday, when her date showed up at Lou's door. Ted was dressed in a black overcoat, leather gloves and black hat. He would have fit right in at Daddy's club.

"Good evening." He offered her his arm to help her down the sidewalk to his sedan. Like him, the dark and serviceable car would fit in anywhere. She wondered if he'd deliberately chosen a vehicle off the least-stolen list.

"I apologize for being late," he said as they started down the street. "The speed limit is thirty-five on every street in this town, and yet I'm behind an idiot who won't go over twenty. I didn't want to pass him because he kept riding the centerline. People like him should have to take a driving test every year."

"Better too slow than too fast," Dorothea offered.

"Oh, no, not according to statistics." She peeked. Ted was going exactly thirty-five. "Drivers going too slow are more apt to cause an accident than those over speed limit. You can look it up."

Time to change the topic.

"May I ask what you have planned?" She already knew, of course.

"The Rotary Club's fish fry is tonight. I believe in supporting the community. The fish will probably be a little overcooked and the tartar sauce is too rich, but it is for a good cause."

The signal went to yellow. Ted hit the brakes throwing Dorothea back against the leather as her seat belt tightened.

"Why they have to put a stop light at every corner, I don't know," he groused. "Things were fine when they had the signs up. Someone's idea of turning us into a big city, I suppose."

Dorothea's good mood was fading fast. The thought of spending the next couple of hours with Mr. Grumpy was depressing. Then again, maybe he'd cheer up when they arrived at the school for dinner.

She wasn't surprised when Ted expressed his unhappiness with having to park near the back of the lot. His diatribe on how one should always park under a light to thwart break-ins continued until they stepped inside the building. Ted pulled two tickets from his wallet and handed them to the Rotarian at the door. Dorothea was surprised he didn't complain about the price. Although, come to think of it, the newspaper had probably taken care of it.

Ted scanned the room before escorting her to a table already occupied by another couple. She was pleased to see that Melinda, the pastor she'd met earlier in the week, was the female half.

"Hello again." Melinda patted the chair next to her. Dorothea waited in vain for Ted to pull out her chair. No such luck. He was already deep into a complaint to her companion about the condition of the parking lot.

The meal that quickly appeared was huge and delicious. The catfish was golden brown, the coleslaw both crisp and creamy, and the accompanying baked beans had a tang she appreciated.

"Well, tonight they finally got it right." Ted took a bite of his fish. "Must have someone new cooking. Dale's done it for years. It's about time he let someone younger take over."

She wasn't surprised when he pronounced the slaw too wet and the beans over-spiced.

No wonder the man wasn't married at nearly forty. His perfect woman couldn't possibly exist.

"Hello there."

She looked up to see Rick behind her. She introduced Ted and Melinda and the man she'd learned was the minister's husband. Rick sat down without waiting for an invitation.

Dorothea held her breath, waiting for her date to gripe about that. Instead, he extended his hand and began to ask Rick questions about himself. This was a whole new Ted.

Eventually the truth dawned on her. The man's business was selling life insurance, and he had a new prospect. She almost giggled. The least likely person in this room to decide he needed a million dollars in coverage was Rick Rahall, the wanderer.

She chatted with Melinda while Ted continued his probing. As she talked about her newfound love of yoga, the buys she'd found at the outlet mall and how excited she was about being the new advice columnist, Dorothea realized how much she liked this new life. She had yet to miss dinners at the club with Daddy, the charity events Patrice scheduled for them or the boring discussions of what to serve when they entertained.

If she hadn't overheard Michael dissecting her flaws, she'd still be stuck in it. Right now, she would be poring over that book of Patrice's and worrying over making a mistake.

Instead, she had freedom. For the first time in her life, she had complete and total control over her own future.

"Here's my card." She realized Ted was talking to her, too. "One for each of you. I'll be glad to sit down with you any time you'd like."

Did she have life insurance already? Dorothea didn't know. Daddy took care of those things, the same way he gave her money and provided a car.

Len showed up for the great picture-taking just as the post-dinner entertainment began. Dorothea had never played bingo before, but she discovered it to be great fun. She was so busy checking her numbers she didn't even notice when Len left.

"We both need the same number." Rick reached over and tapped her card.

"I won't win. I never do." Ted was glum. Big surprise.

A cry of *Bingo!* cheated both Dorothea and Rick from a victory. She won the next game, though, and received a ten-dollar gift card from the local gas station as her prize.

"That won't get you much the way fuel prices are," Ted commented.

Dorothea met Rick's eyes and bit her lip to keep from laughing. They definitely shared the same thought.

Ted doggedly stuck it out to the end despite griping every time someone else called out the magic word. He was persistent; she had to give him that. He was also polite, walking her to the door before reminding her that everyone needed to worry about their final expenses.

Rick was already sitting in the foyer with Lou and a carafe of coffee. Warmed by the fire, they took turns telling their hostess about the evening and especially the bingo extravaganza.

"I bombed out entirely, but Dixie won ten bucks in gas," Rick said. "She's beautiful and lucky, too, the perfect combination."

He thought she was pretty? No one had ever seriously said that about her before. Being told she had a classic look or that her skin had a glow were the highest compliments any man had ever paid her. Beautiful, Rick had called her. Wow.

"I'd love to hear more, but it's past my bedtime," Lou said. She poked the fire before bidding them goodnight. Dorothea remained curled on the divan, her feet tucked beneath her, and sighed. Life was good.

Rick stared into the fire. He cradled his cup with both hands, something she noticed he did often. Funny how she knew that about him already, the same way she knew he ate all of one food first before tasting the next. She couldn't remember how Michael ate except he always seemed to have a glass of something strong beside his plate.

"So what's next for you?"

Dorothea froze. He knew. Somehow he'd discovered she was only a pretender, that Dixie White would cease to exist as easily as she had come into being.

"Do you pick the best date or something?"

Oh. Rick meant...

"The whole town's invited to meet my dates and me on Valentine's Day. I understand there will be refreshments, door prizes, things like that. It should be fun."

"Think you'll be seeing any of those guys again?"

Dorothea wasn't an expert at body language, but she was sure the way he leaned forward and tipped his head meant something. Like her romantic future might be resting on her answer.

"They're all nice guys, but I didn't click with any of them. I suspect it will be the same with the last one."

"But you're not opposed to a relationship?"

Rick was definitely asking for his own reasons. She mimicked his pose, leaning toward him as she said with Dixie's boldness, "Sure, with the right guy. He'd have to love to dance and be open to adventure."

"Ah." Rick grinned. "Of course, you wouldn't be interested in dating someone like that until after you've broken those guys' hearts, I suppose."

"One must be polite."

"Another trait I admire in a woman."

He rose to shift a fallen log back into place. Dorothea wasn't sure whether the sudden warmth she felt was from the fire or a result of Rick's forwardness. She did know, though, she was treading on new ground. Her limited experience with dating had been the result of someone else's actions. Even Michael had been a fix-up, encouraged by her father when he took a liking to his new hire. Dinner at the country club for the three of them had ended up being just two when Daddy slipped out early.

Ah, well, Dixie would know what to do.

****

An unfamiliar emotion assailed Rick as he stepped out the back door of the big Victorian house with the small cottage as his destination. Lou was headed for a church women's meeting, and Dixie was on her final date. He knew they'd be gone a couple of hours at least. That should give him time for a quick look-see.

Guilt. That's why he stopped with his fingers on the door handle Dixie left unlocked. But it wasn't like he was going through her underwear drawer, he told himself. He'd just look at things she'd left out. Like mail, maybe. Or a credit card with Dorothea Pfister's name on it. The easiest thing to do was haul himself down to the This and That and flat out ask Charlie who used that infuriating piece of plastic. Rick's excuse to himself was he didn't want to put Dixie's reputation in jeopardy if someone else had used it.

He took a deep breath, turned the handle and stepped in.

She was neat. The place smelled good too. He looked around and spotted a jar candle.

Picking it up, he checked the scent. Warm vanilla. Like cookies.

Nothing was out of place, not even on the desk he could tell was her workspace. A closed laptop took center stage. A cup decorated with butterflies held pens, pencils and scissors with red handles. Two manila envelopes were stacked on each other, one horizontal and one vertical. He read her neat labels: *To do* and *Done*. Must be the letters the newspaper got in.

Rick pulled the center drawer open. Paper clips, tape, a little packet of rubber bands.

Maybe they were hers; maybe the last user had left them there. Nothing looked out of place.

The three small drawers to the right of the kneehole were all empty. He glanced around the room trying to figure out where she might put stolen credit cards. Or stolen anything else.

Thieves tended to keep piling up illicit items until they were caught.

The kitchen cabinets held a tiny bit of snack food, tea bags and hot beverage mixes. She was a regular at the diner, just like him. He often saw her arriving when he was leaving.
Apparently she ate late.

The yoga mat propped by the door was the only personal item in plain sight. But she might have chosen the garage as a better hiding place.

Once again he hesitated before entering. What if someone saw him and told Dixie he'd been poking around? This was a small town. People talked.

But back in Chicago, three people were desperately seeking Dorothea. He went in through the side door.
And there was the Saab he'd been looking for. He read the license plate. The numbers were a match for those he'd memorized.

Dorothea's car, which Dixie never drove.

With a sinking heart, he tried the passenger door. It easily opened. He sniffed. The interior smelled like freshener spray. He took a deeper breath. If it covered the smell of death and decay, he wasn't catching it.

Rick found the interior trunk latch. The trunk lid lifted. He walked around for an inspection and found only a pair of snow boots and a spare tire in its assigned place.

If Dorothea was dead, she hadn't been in the Saab.

He closed the trunk and left the garage, his mind whirling. Could Dorothea be Dixie?

His conversations with the missing woman's friends confirmed everything he'd already been told. Put bluntly, Dorothea Pfister was dull.

Dixie White was anything but. Dixie grabbed life with both hands, open to new experiences. Victor's little girl would never go on a blind date, let alone seven of them. She wouldn't tour a distillery with a stranger. She'd never tour a distillery period. She wouldn't wear used clothes and presume to give advice to others. She certainly wouldn't curl against him as they danced—her head against his shoulder as if they belonged together.

He slammed his fist against a tree trunk. The Dixie he knew, the one he was starting to like very much, wasn't a thief. She didn't use other people's credit cards or steal cars. She was honest, an open book.

Except Dixie White had no past. Everyone left some sort of electronic footprint, but she had no bank accounts, no social media accounts, not even a record of a cell phone. He had to accept the impossible.

The woman he was searching for had been under his nose this whole time. Dorothea wasn't hospitalized or hiding away in a high-class hotel. She was playing at being someone else right here in Cardington.

What was her game?

Chapter Nine

The heated leather seats were heavenly. The ride of the upscale car was one of the smoothest Dorothea had ever experienced. If only she could roll down a window, everything would be fine. She suspected that sticking her head into a cool winter's evening and breathing deeply might insult Biff Salliman. She was almost willing to chance spending the night with an angry date rather than continue to be assaulted by his musk-heavy cologne and what she swore smelled like hair spray.

He'd greeted her with a firm handshake and a car-shaped refrigerator magnet she tucked in her purse.

"We're a full-service auto store," he said as he handed it over. "Oil changes, tune-ups, tires, whatever you need." He winked. "I'll give you a nice discount."

Although the schedule had said *private dinner*, Dorothea didn't expect it to be in the showroom of Salliman Motors. Biff pulled up to a wide glass door and parked. He opened her door, offered his arm and escorted her in. A table covered with crisp linens had been set with crystal goblets, china and silver spoons and forks.

A pair of young women in white shirts and short black skirts brought out a napkin-wrapped bottle of wine and a tray of appetizers. Dorothea surveyed them with delight: stuffed mushroom caps, delicate shrimp, rounds of toast topped with goat's cheese. She certainly didn't expect this.

"That's how you do it," Biff said with a satisfied smile when she complimented him on the choices. "We're not all a bunch of hicks here."

"You're not a Cardington native, are you?"

"Started life in Michigan, grew up in Pittsburgh and moved here to make my wife happy. Now she's my ex-wife, lives about twenty miles away, and I've got the biggest used car business in three counties. Eat up. You're going to love the rest of the meal."

She'd almost forgotten the purpose of the evening until Len showed up. He winked and stole a canapé.

"No dinner yet," he offered as an excuse. "I can't believe you're eating like this, and I'll be stuck with roller food from the convenience store when I'm finally done. Now why don't you two pose over by that convertible?"

The courses that followed Len's departure were fabulous. A delicate salad with raspberry vinaigrette began the meal. Next came tender pork loin slices, tiny new red potatoes, asparagus with a hollandaise sauce, and light yeast rolls with true butter.

"That was fantastic." Dorothea relaxed in her chair with a cup of rich dark-roasted coffee.

"We still have dessert," Biff reminded her. "I don't know about you, but I wouldn't mind a little ride before we enjoy that."

Dorothea might have asked for a destination and questioned his intent. Dixie stood up and said, "That sounds like fun."

She was stunned when he grabbed a set of keys from a board and led her around the building to a sleek black vehicle.

"You sell Jags?" she asked. She couldn't imagine there was a huge demand for them in Cardington.

"I'll sell this one if someone comes up with the money. Mostly I drive it around for fun."

Being with Biff in that car sent her back into her recent past, to the world of men who talked business and loved to show off what they'd accomplished. Once again, she felt like window dressing while he made a slow trip through town before heading out on the open road to show what the car could do. By the time they arrived back to the showroom for dessert, she knew his profit margin, that he was to be the grand marshal of the town's

Memorial Day parade and how sorry his ex-wives were to have lost him.

Champagne and cheesecake with a raspberry topping waited for them. The evening would be perfect if she was with someone else.

Like Rick.

She pushed the thought away. She had committed to this date, and Biff deserved her full attention while she was with him. Granted that consisted mostly of nodding and saying, "I see." Stroking this guy's ego was pretty easy.

Biff was one happy man, she decided on the way back to Lou's. His supreme selfconfidence, obvious willingness to indulge his hobbies and love of fine cuisine might be a bit much for her, but his perfect woman must be out there somewhere.

"That's how you do it," he said, repeating the phrase he'd used at least a dozen times during their date. "Find the best, hire them and enjoy yourself. Life's short. You gotta make the best of it."

He hesitated as he escorted her up the sidewalk toward the door.

"I know the rules," he said, "but if you're not against a good night kiss..."

"Can't break the rules." She kept her rebuke light. "I have enjoyed the evening, though."

"Call if you want to do it again." Biff started moving again. "Next time I'll really pull out the stops."

Dorothea refrained from mentioning that there would be no next time. She had no intention of bursting his balloon. If Biff wanted to believe he was God's gift to women, she'd let him keep his delusion.

****

"Have a good time?" Lou asked.

"Not as good as Biff had," Dorothea answered. "He didn't need me to enjoy his evening."

Her remark brought a rich laugh from Rick and a chuckle from Lou. She described the food, with interruptions from Lou who wanted details, and gave details on the Jaguar particularly for Rick.

"No wonder you're a writer," Rick said when she finished. "You have a real way of telling a story."

"Thank you." His words warmed Dorothea.

"We're lucky you decided to settle here," Lou said. "Len's tickled to death to have new blood at the paper. The women's circle down at church wants to invite you to our next meeting, by the way. We're going to be baking cookies for the folks who get noon meals delivered to them."

Guilt pressed on Dorothea. She almost confessed her ruse. But the thought of having these two turn against her made her selfish. She wasn't ready to give up what she'd found with these two special people.

"That sounds like a great project," she said. "I'll see if I can make it."

"You don't have any other place to be, do you?"

Rick's question made her guilt into a palpable feeling, pressing against her heart and making her stomach clench. She was sure Lou would forgive her for her lies. She was uncertain of Rick's reaction. That moment when they'd danced, their give-and-take conversations, the vibe she felt when he was near—she was certain he also felt the chemistry. It was too soon to test their tentative connection.

"Maybe I'm a rolling stone like you." She tried to keep her answer light. "Wanderlust might overtake me at any time."

"Not until you get all those letters answered." Lou waved a hand toward the mantel. "Len dropped some more off right after you left."

"More?"

"You've become quite popular. It seems like everyone in town has seen you one place or another. I'd say you're our new celebrity." She laughed. "Not that we have any in Cardington. It's a pretty easy title to win."

Lou left her companions by the fire as had become her habit. The fire cast shadows on Rick's face, adding a sternness that made it impossible for

Dorothea to keep her secret. She had to tell him the truth.

"Can I tell you something?" she asked.

"Sure." Rick looked up and met her eyes. "Anything you'd like."

"Dixie White is my nom de plume, my writing name." Dorothea took a deep breath and kept going. "My name is actually Dorothea Pfister. My family thinks I'm on vacation in Florida. No one has any idea that I'm here or that I write my column."

"Is there a reason you didn't want to use your real name?"

"No. Yes." Dorothea shook her head. "You wouldn't understand."

"Try me," Rick said.

His voice was gentle, almost sympathetic, and opened the floodgates. She told him about the engagement she didn't know how to break, the life of doing nothing of importance and her confusion over her future. She poured out her feelings of inadequacy and her worry over her father's reaction if she refused to go through with marriage to Michael.

"Do you hate me now?" she asked.

The quiet question was unexpected. After his visit to the garage and discovery of the Saab, Rick had planned to confront Dixie tonight. She preempted him by baring her soul and putting him smack into the biggest dilemma of his life. He had to choose between revealing her location to his client or giving this woman a chance to become all she wanted to be.

He couldn't make a snap decision.

"I could never hate you," he said. "I have a confession of my own."

"Oh?" He watched her steel herself. She straightened in her chair and folded her hands in her lap. Rick was watching her transform into the perfect lady who never showed emotion.

"Your father hired me to find you."

Her face tightened; there was no other movement.

"I'm here because your credit card was used. When I first met you, I thought you'd stolen the card. Tonight when I saw your car in the garage, I wondered if you took that too."

"And if I killed the real owner?" Rick shook his head.

"Nah, I couldn't imagine you as a killer." "Nice to know I draw the line at fraud and identity theft."

Rick laughed. She relaxed at the sound, the stranger Dorothea fading back into the Dixie he knew.

"Are you going to call my father?" she asked.

"Not yet. Your note seemed to reassure him. I suggest you call whoever takes care of your place in Florida and let them know you'll be down in a week or two. They'll tell your father, and he'll stop worrying."

He fell silent, waiting for a response that didn't come.

Dixie didn't know what to do either.

"When is this newspaper shindig?" he finally asked.

"Saturday."

"Four days away."

"Four days," she agreed.

Rick was all about compromises, so he offered one.

"I won't tell your dad if you promise to call him once the Valentine's event is over."

Dorothea hesitated for a long minute before agreeing. She stood, said a quiet good night and left him. He waited until he heard the closing of the back door to spread the fire and go up to the blue room that had begun to feel like his.

Rick wondered if she'd sleep tonight. He was pretty certain he wouldn't.

****

At three in the morning, after reading all the new letters and answering a few of the last batch, Dorothea gave up trying not to think about Rick's revelation and the bargain he offered. She should have known this house of cards would fall down around her. The truth was easy to keep track of.

Falsehoods were complicated, especially for someone like her who made a practice of not lying.

She had to tell Len and deal with the fallout. The man took her at her word and hired her without a background check. All those men she'd been out with would wonder why she hid her identity, too. What a mess she'd made.

It occurred to her she had to clean up this mess herself. Daddy's money and Patrice's contacts couldn't help her. Rick's offer was all she had: Four days to fix everything.

She woke up several hours later feeling more rested than she should. The worries of the night seemed smaller now that the sun was shining. She took a shower, fixed some tea and ate a few grapes and fresh mozzarella for breakfast. Ten minutes later, she was sitting across the messy desk from Len.

She made her confession in as succinct and organized a manner as she could. Len's reaction was not what she expected. He began smiling halfway through and was grinning when she finished.

"I wondered who you were." He tapped the top of his computer. "Believe it or not, we check folks out when we hire them. I couldn't find a single piece of information on Dixie White. If you'd come in for a regular position instead of freelancing as a columnist, it might have been a problem. I don't have to worry about your Social Security number or personal information since I just cut you a check. I figured you'd tell me sooner or later."

"You hired me anyway."

"Had to once I read your columns. This paper needs a little freshening up, and you're the ticket. The big question is whether you're going to run out on me."

"Oh, no." Dorothea's tension eased when she realized he wasn't about to fire her. "I love being Dixie White. No matter where I am, I want to keep on writing."

"So go to it. I want a piece for Thursday's paper summing up your dating experience. Something light and fluffy."

"Okay." She could do that.

"By tomorrow afternoon. You can come down here and work if you want. We've got space."

Dorothea stopped by the diner on her way back to Lou's. She placed a to-go order for two servings of peach cobbler, ice cream on the side, and a large coffee with cream and sugar. She carried home the desserts in one large bag and sipped her drink as she walked.

Lou was vacuuming in the downstairs hall when she arrived at the house. As soon as the sweeper cut off, Dorothea held up the bag and asked Lou to join her in the kitchen.

"Oh, my, this looks delicious," Lou said when the treat was placed in front of her. "Is it a special occasion?"

"Not exactly." Dorothea sat down across from her with her own cobbler and ice cream. "I need to tell you something."

"Oh, dear, one of those men hasn't been bothering you, has he?"

"No. This is of a more personal nature."

Lou leaned forward and for a moment, Dorothea wondered if she expected the sort of sordid tale from her afternoon talk shows.

"My name is really Dorothea Pfister, I'm from Chicago, and I'm engaged to a guy I can't stand. I sort of ran away because I didn't know how to get rid of him."

"Is that all?"

Dorothea thought it was a pretty big deal. But of course, she hadn't heard as many fantastic stories as her TV-watching landlady.

"My father thinks I went to Florida to our place down there. He hired a detective to find me."

"No one's going to look for you in Cardington."

"He already has. It's Rick."

"Oh, my."

Now Lou looked surprised. Dorothea wondered if it was because she wasn't sure about having a detective in the house or if Lou found this a fantastic turn of events. Dorothea added details, explaining the surprise engagement, her sudden decision not to go to Florida, and how much she loved Cardington.

"Living in a city like Chicago is so different." Dorothea tried to find the right words.

"Here everyone knows each other. Back home, I barely know the people living next to us. I mean, I do if going to the same restaurants and country club counts. But I never sat around a fireplace to share cookies like we do."

"Cities have lots of neighborhoods," Lou replied, "while here we just have one. You know how it is. Blink while you're driving and you'll miss downtown. The whole couple blocks of it."

Dorothea pushed on, driven by a jumble of emotions.

"I wanted to go to college in New Mexico and study art," she confessed. "Daddy worried I'd get homesick so far from the Midwest. Patrice told me I couldn't support myself with paintings and pottery because that takes talent I don't have. And like she said, my father wants grandchildren to carry on the family, and there's no one but me to give them to him."

"What do you want?"

No one had ever asked her that before. Her path in life had been pre-destined thanks to her family name and expectations. No wonder Michael envisioned her as a means to his ends.

"I should have said no," she said.

Lou frowned.

"To what, dear?"

"To Michael Butterwell for sure. But Daddy had such excitement on his face, and everyone important was staring at us. I couldn't make a scene. But now look at the mess I'm in."

She stopped, teary-eyed.

"Oh, sweetie." Lou quickly rounded the table to wrap her arms around Dorothea who leaned into them. She couldn't remember the last time she'd been comforted like this. Pfisters were strong and stoic.

Cobbler and a good cry did a lot to restore Dorothea's equilibrium. She went to the yoga class she planned to skip and returned feeling much better about herself and the situation. Rick had agreed to give her four days. She intended to make the best use of them she could before she faced her father.

Chapter Ten

Dorothea drove to the newspaper office the next morning. The weather had changed to a just-at-freezing chill. Rather than chance icy sidewalks, she piled what she needed into the car. Her laptop, of course, since she was producing that story for Len. Her journal with the notes about the dates. For the first time in her life, she also packed a lunch. The money she brought with her from Chicago was running low. If she was careful, she could make it until her first paycheck next week.

She knew it was ridiculous to let such a small amount of money excite her. She made more working for Daddy's friends. But she always regarded those jobs as favors to her father rather than an appreciation of her abilities.

"Good morning," she sang as she walked in and greeted Stella.

"Well, someone's in a good mood." Stella leaned back in her chair and studied her with narrowed eyes. "New boyfriend, maybe?" Dorothea laughed.

"They're all nice guys but absolutely zero connection."

"There is another new guy in town." Stella wiggled her eyebrows suggestively.

Dorothea felt her face warm. She was *not* going to talk about Rick.

"Maybe I just woke up in a good mood," she suggested.

"Maybe. Len's out right now."

"That's okay. If you can point me to a desk, I'd appreciate it. He wants me to write a short piece on my experience."

She was soon sitting at a well-used metal desk at the back of the room. A stack of old newspapers occupied one corner. Dorothea used the rest. She jotted notes on a yellow legal pad Stella supplied, capturing the more memorable moments of the last seven evenings.

This writing thing turned out to be more challenging than she had expected. She knew what she wanted to create—a light, breezy account of a single girl in the world of blind dates.

Her first attempts sounded more like an anthropological study. She finally realized why.

Dorothea had her hands on the keys, not Dixie.

Shoving everything out of her mind except the last week, she began to type. She wrote and rewrote until she was satisfied with the results. She e-mailed the story to Len, who still hadn't come in, and switched to her column. She should be able to get several done before the time limit was up.

Rick had appeared for their nightly ritual of a snack and coffee the evening before, a few hours after her great confession to Lou. No one mentioned her double life. Instead, they discussed everything from whether tattoos were really art to new movies coming out. Even after Lou excused herself, Rick avoided the subject of Dorothea versus Dixie.

Now there were only three days. A mere seventy-two hours until the Valentine's Day whoop-de-do was over and she had to call Daddy. Maybe she should let Rick make his report and let things happen as they would. She was an adult. She didn't have to report to anyone. But she did have more columns to write.

Dear Dixie,

My wife has one annoying habit: She never lets me finish a sentence. If we go out for dinner, she'll order my beverage before I have a chance to. If I'm telling a story about something that happened, she cuts me off. We've been married for twenty-five years and I love her, but she's driving me crazy. Help!

Desperate Hubby

That poor man. Dorothea couldn't imagine putting up with not finishing a sentence for a quarter of a century. She put his letter aside to mull over and moved on to the next one. Len came in, said hello and went to his desk to read her story. He offered some small suggestions, which she made before he left again.

The afternoon was nearly over before Dorothea's shoulders ached and her eyes glazed over. She wasn't used to spending so much time at a computer. She wondered how Stella could do it all day long.

"Do you need help with anything for Saturday?" she asked as she passed the other woman's desk.

"We're in great shape," Stella said. "Food's ordered, my sister is going to help me decorate, and the men all say they'll be there. You just need to show up and be pretty. I think we'll have lots of folks there. Maybe they'll subscribe to the newspaper too."

The days seemed to fly by. Dorothea found the perfect party dress at New to You. One of Lou's friends made the necessary alterations and by Saturday morning, Dorothea had nothing left to do but think. She'd received numerous compliments on her little story with assurances from nearly everyone at the diner and in her yoga class that they'd be there.

****

Rick studied himself in the mirror. He rarely dressed up except for weddings and funerals. He'd run over to the mall to pick up a blazer, pale blue shirt and dark blue tie for the occasion, pairing them with khakis. Good enough, he decided.

"Ready?"

He turned to see a barely recognizable Lou. Her accustomed slacks and pullover shirts had been abandoned for a dress and jacket with sparkles on them. She was even wearing high heels.

"As ready as I'll ever be," he said.

"Good. Our girl's waiting downstairs."

He walked into the foyer and stopped cold, barely able to breathe. Dixie was gorgeous. Her hair was different, pulled over to the side somehow with a little spray of roses. She wore a fluffy red dress with a full skirt that stopped just above her knee and a snug bodice. Long slim legs ended in shimmering red pumps. Hanging diamond earrings caught the glimmer of firelight.

There was no way this beautiful creature was the plain and placid Dorothea. This was Dixie in all her glory.

"Do I look all right?" she asked, hesitant.

"Beautiful." Rick smiled and came closer to tuck an errant strand of hair behind her ear. "Incredible."

He wanted to kiss those red lips. Might have if Lou hadn't been there.

"Do you have post-party plans?" he asked.

Dixie shook her head.

"Would you care to go to dinner with me?"

"I'd love to."

Rick hadn't meant to ask her out. Seeing her, though, he knew he wanted to spend time with her alone before she went back to Chicago and a life that had no room for someone like him. Michael would probably look better to her back at home, wedding plans would progress, and he'd become someone she once met and then forgot.

He wouldn't forget her.

****

The fire department meeting room was a tribute to Cupid's powers. Red was the predominant color with hearts everywhere. As Len suggested, Dixie arrived fashionably late in order to make an entrance. Applause and cheers greeted her as she walked in with Lou and Rick behind her.

While she posed for pictures and visited with her many admirers, Rick found the fountain of pink punch. He sipped the sweet liquid as he watched Dixie in action. Even though he knew who she really was, he still had trouble believing it. Maybe he'd escort Dorothea to her loving father himself. He'd love to see the look on Patrice's face when this radiant, assured creature walked in. Butterwell would probably be too sloshed to react.

Lou was like a butterfly, flitting here and there. Rick was content to stay in a corner as an observer. He made small talk when people came up to him, but they seldom stayed long. He was eager for this to be over. He wanted Dixie all to himself.

He'd known her, what, three weeks and he could already imagine what she'd be like at Christmas. She'd insist on sitting on Santa's lap to have her picture taken when they went to the mall. She'd start snowball fights and hold her cold hands to his cheeks to make him yell.

Except it wasn't going to happen. He'd only have memories of her wrinkling her nose at the distillery smell, her amusing recaps of those blind dates and the way she was tonight.

Rather than ending, the party tapered off. Soon no one was left but the newspaper staff, Lou, Rick and, of course, Dixie herself. She came over, shoes in hand, and took the punch cup from Rick's hand.

"I am dying of thirst." She nearly drained the cup before handing it back to him. "And starving."

"We'll take care of that, too. We have reservations."

He was quietly grateful when Len offered to take Lou home. Selfish man that he was, he wanted every moment alone with Dixie that he could steal. He'd chosen Parker's, even though it had been the site of one of her dates, because it was the closest classy place.

Rick hadn't been on a real date in a long time. Keeping up a relationship when you did late-night stakeouts and never knew when you'd be in town was impossible. He did remember, though, that women love romance—especially on Valentine's Day.

"Your wine, sir."

The steward produced the bottle and poured a bit into Rick's glass for him to sample. At a nod of approval, he filled both glasses. Dixie raised her glass and said, "Shall we toast?" Rick smiled and lifted his own.

"To beautiful women and bright futures," he said.

"And handsome men with good hearts," she added.

The evening was perfect from that moment on. The food was excellent, the musicians quite talented. Rick felt a rapport with this woman that went beyond similar likes. He almost felt like she was the woman he had known would come into his life sometime.

Dixie seemed to feel the same way. She was witty, quick with quips and retorts. They laughed, they talked, they shared snippets of their lives that cemented the bond he felt. All too soon, they finished their desserts and it was time to leave.

"I had a wonderful time." Dixie held his arm and leaned against him as they walked to his car. "I'll never forget this night. Or you."

She stopped on those last words and moved her hand to his shoulders. Standing on her toes, Dixie kissed his lips. Rick accepted the invitation and returned the kiss, his arms pulling her close. He didn't care who saw them. He only cared about the taste of her, the feel of her soft breasts against his chest, the way her breathing quickened.

He wanted her. He was certain she wanted him. Since they were two consenting adults, he was fairly sure the night would end in her cottage, in her bed.

"Let's go home," she whispered against him. Those three small words confirmed his assumption.

The moon was a mere sliver in the sky tonight, not the romantic full moon that inspired poets. Rick drove the curves of the access road with Dixie's hand in his, neither of them speaking. He put both hands on the wheel when they approached the interstate.

A car with bright headlights came toward them. Rick braked, expecting the driver to cut in front of him and onto the highway. The car kept coming, sliding across the dividing line, heading straight for them.

Rick clutched the wheel and steered hard to the right to avoid a collision. He heard Dixie's gasp as the other car kept coming toward them and then, as metal ground into metal, felt the world spin and go black.

****

Dixie moaned and clutched her chest. The seat belt was an iron sash, pressing down, burning against her. The exploded air bag was her enemy as she struggled to move. Brilliant headlights blinded her; she closed her eyes until she saw black against her eyelids again.

Opening them to a tiny slit, she looked over at Rick.

He wasn't moving.

"Rick!" she called his name, reached out to touch his face and felt something sticky beneath her fingers. His air bag covered him as well. A disembodied voice came from the speaker of the still running car. Relief flooded through her as she told the On-Star operator that yes, there had been an accident. And no, they weren't all right. The operator stayed with her, reassuring Dixie, until first responders arrived in a flood of blue and red lights and a sea of sirens.

"Take care of him," she screamed when the EMTs started to get her out.

"We are," came the calm voice of her red-haired rescuer. "Right now we need to take care of you."

"No! Take care of him. I'm all right," she repeated over and over.

Dixie finally let the woman do a quick examination, lift her from the seat and answered the EMT's questions. But all the time she was screaming inside, certain Rick was dying. Or maybe already dead.

"Let me stay," she begged as the EMTs carried her to an ambulance. "He needs to go first."

"There's a paramedic with him now," the redhead assured her. "See that other ambulance? They'll take him, and we'll take you. You can see him in the hospital, but now we have to go."

Only after they left the scene did Dorothea realize her shoulder hurt badly and her knee throbbed. She'd been hurt a little. Just a little when Rick...

Tears began to roll down her face. The EMT leaned over and said, "We're almost there.

They'll give you something for pain as soon as we arrive."

Dorothea didn't bother to correct her. The tears were for Rick. And for what might have been and perhaps never would be.

The unit carrying Rick was already at the emergency room bay when they pulled in. She caught a glimpse of him on a fast-rolling gurney pushed by the blue-uniformed rescuers. He was in a curtained triage area by the time she arrived at another mini-room further down the hall.

The jostling made her shoulder pain more intense. Amid a blur of nurses and doctors, she felt a poke in her arm, saw a bag of clear fluid hung on an IV pole and then nothing but oblivion as the pain medicine kicked in. Her last thought before she went under entirely was a prayer, a fervent hope Rick still lived.

Chapter Eleven

Dorothea forced her eyes open and immediately let the lids fall back down against the offending light. She heard noise around her but groggy and confused, she couldn't decide where she was. Not in her little cottage and most certainly not home with Daddy.

"Miss White?"

The voice came to her from underwater, blurred and barely audible.

"Dixie? You need to wake up now."

She tried opening her eyes again and managed by looking toward the floor, not straight up. From above a pair of white shoes and white cotton pants, the voice came again.

"Your surgery went fine. We'll be moving you to a room as soon as you stay awake and drink something for me, okay?"

What a stupid dream. I have to wake up.

She reached up to slap her face but something got in the way. Plastic tubing, a metal rail...what happened to her?

"I'm going to put you up now."

The bed beneath her moved and her head went up. She forced her gaze up and saw a nurse looking back at her. Oh God. She was in the hospital. A car had missed the exit, smashed into them and...

"Where's Rick?" she croaked.

"He's in another room."

"How's Rick?"

The nurse's hesitation was more answer than the subsequent words.

"Holding his own. You can see him when you're a little better."

More nurses then, more questions, the insistence that she drink. Dorothea tolerated it because they wouldn't leave her alone. Next came the strange ride through the hospital halls to a room and finally the sweet release of drugs that plunged her back into sleep.

The next day was an unending cycle of wakefulness and sedation. On the third day, she stayed awake longer and traded morphine for pain pills. She also got to see Rick.

The nurse's aide who helped her into a wheelchair and took her to him was sweet but not forthcoming with details. Dixie was shocked when the aide wheeled her into Rick's room to see him unmoving and with a respirator attached. A doctor and nurse stood at the foot of his bed.

"Tell me what's wrong," she begged.

"Ah, you're the young lady who was in the car with him."

"Yes." She hissed the word. "Tell me how he is."

"He has a broken leg and some internal injuries so we're keeping him deeply sedated to give him a chance to heal."

"But he's going to be all right, isn't he?" The doctor's face was grave.

"Right now we're giving him time to heal," he repeated. "We'll know more in a few days. I think perhaps you need to rest as well."

The aide recognized the dismissal and took Dorothea back down the hall to her own private room. Getting back into bed was a painful and exhausting struggle. But before she took another pain pill, Dorothea had something to do.

"Can you dial a number for me?" She gestured at the phone on the table by her bed. "Just reverse the charges. He'll take a collect call."

The young woman dialed the number before handing over the receiver. Dorothea listened to the rings, four in succession, and spoke when a familiar voice said, "Pfister here."

"Daddy," she said, "I need you."

"Dorothea, baby, are you all right? Where have you been? Why haven't you called?" She cut in, determined to say what she had to while she still had the strength.

"There was an accident. I'm in a hospital, but I'm okay. Daddy, Rick isn't. You need to come. Right now."

Exhausted, she handed the phone back to the aide to give details and directions. When the medicine kicked in, she willingly gave herself up to the dark. Her father was coming. He'd make the doctors fix Rick. Her father could do anything.

****

When she woke again it was dark outside, and a large figure filled the chair by her bed.

"Daddy?"

"Oh, baby, I'm right here." Victor came over, sat on the edge of the bed and held the hand attached to the uninjured arm. "Thank God you're okay. You had a dislocated shoulder, but they've taken care of that. You're going to be good as new."

"Rick," she protested. "What about Rick?"

"He's better. Let's just worry about you."

"No. Don't try to shelter me. Tell me the truth."

Victor looked down at their joined hands, then at the floor. Finally he spoke, as if he'd just made up his mind.

"He had emergency surgery early this morning, but they think he'll be all right. His doctor said they're going to start waking him up today."

"Good."

She knew her father was dying to ask questions. He wanted to know every detail, and he wanted to know it now. Here, though, they were on her turf. He had to wait until she was ready.

That moment came a few days later when she was ready for discharge and Rick was fully awake. She and her father sat in Rick's room to start the discussion she really didn't want to have.

"First of all, I didn't run away," she said. "I couldn't bear to be in the house, and you didn't want me to go to Miami alone. My intention was to go to the airport and catch a flight. But I turned the other way, ended up in Cardington, got a job and learned there's a whole lot to life that I've never known.

"Rick really didn't know I was Dixie. Or rather, that Dixie was me. We're not much alike, Dixie and me. And quite honestly, I think I'd rather be the woman I am here."

Victor scrubbed his hand across his face.

"Michael's been beside himself with worry," he said, "and Patrice was nearly frantic."

"But neither of them bothered to come with you."

"Michael's getting ready for a big trial and Patrice is getting things in place for when you come home, rescheduling the engagement photo until you're healed."

"That's something else we have to talk about," Dorothea said. "I'm not marrying Michael. He thinks I'm frumpy and a brood cow. And if I come back home, Patrice can forget about scheduling my life. I can do that myself."

"When we get you home and all that medicine's out of your system, you'll be your old self again," he said. "You'll realize how much they care for you."

Rick and Dorothea exchanged glances. They both knew Michael and Patrice would be more likely to throw a party if she stayed away than mourn her absence.

"I've thought about this quite a bit," Dorothea said, "and I believe I may be better suited to life here. After all, I have a residence and a job and what more do I really need?"

She waited for her father to protest. She already knew all the arguments by heart. At one time she would have given in. Not now. Not since her experiences in Cardington had shown her another way to live.

"What about you, Rick?" Victor looked as if he wanted an ally. "Don't you think she'd be better off in Chicago?"

"I think she should do whatever she wants. With whoever she wants." Victor threw up his hands.

"So you're taking her side?"

"This isn't a war, sir." Rick cleared his throat and spoke louder. "You fought and made the life you wanted. You have a woman back there who would love to share it. You need to let Dorothea make her own choices, the way you did."

"Dammit, man."

"She won't be alone if she stays. I'll be around until I'm healed, which the doctor says could be a couple of months."

"And she'll be perfectly safe with me."

All three turned to look at the speaker who stood in the doorway with a basket of muffins.

"We love our Dixie," Lou said, "and since Rick's going to be staying with me as well, there will be two of us she can call on. Now how about we declare a truce and have some of my blueberry muffins?"

When Lou winked, Dorothea knew it would be all right. Her father might have his own ideas of propriety and conduct, but he did want what was best for her. She knew what that was.

The chance of her life's love with Rick, a real job that was so much fun and an entire town that she could call family.

THE END

Dear Reader:

I hope you enjoyed Dorothea's adventures as much as I did. While none of her dates were based on real people, I must admit that certain traits from individuals I've known were adapted to add life to a few of the men who took the challenge of dating Dixie. The town of Cardington only exists in my imagination, but it is based on the wonderful small towns in which I have lived and worked over the decades of my life.

Lou's house is modeled on the brick Victorian home of my late parents. Some of the best evenings of my life were spent sitting by the foyer fireplace with a cup of coffee and whatever treats my mother had tucked away in the kitchen. She made the best chocolate chip cookies ever!

Cat

ABOUT CAT SHAFFER

Cat lives in the peaceful hills of eastern Kentucky where life is easy. Critics praise her small town settings and vivid characters, which are a product of a lifetime in rural communities and tiny towns. She shares her home with a dog and a cat, which creates some lively moments.

The daughter of a poet and a schoolteacher, Cat learned to read before she went to school and began writing as soon as she learned to form letters. Her first writing award came in fourth grade and set her on the path to doing what she loves. Visit Cat's website for more about her and her books.
http://www.catshaffer.com

Other books by Cat include:
Kentucky Blues
No Safe Place
Bittersweet
Her Hired Man
Man of Her Dreams

If you enjoyed Cat Shaffer's *Dixie White and the Seven Dates* please consider telling others and writing a review.

www.ingramcontent.com/pod-product-compliance
Lightning Source LLC
Chambersburg PA
CBHW061231170626
46809CB00007B/2620